PUFFIN

Seriously Sassy

Pinch me, I'm dreaming

Hey! Here it is, my second book – woop woop! So, what's up? Well, **Cordelia** and **Tas** are still the **best bezzies** ever. OK, so Cordelia freaks me out sometimes when her green eyes flash in that **spooky** way. And Taslima thinks my whole family **are nuts**! But I'm SO glad they're both around.

Megan's still lurking. Magnus too. Which bothers me a bit! And then there's Twig, who can hang around as much as he wants . . .

But mostly this book's about my **BIG DREAM**. You know, getting my music out there. And I was thinking, maybe you have a **BIG DREAM** too?

Like, maybe you want to be a **singer**, an Olympic athlete, a **hot-shot** lawyer, a brilliant scientist or whatever.

Or maybe you've got a massive **CRUSH** on someone you think will **NEVER EVER** notice you!

Well, don't give up! Cos sometimes dreams CAN come true. Even if it's in the way you least expect – I should know! Read on and you'll find out why . . .

Sassy X

PS Pip sends a big **mwah-mwah kiss** too!

THANK YOU to . . .

Maggi would like to thank all those who helped this book become more than just a dream. Her brilliant editor, Amanda. Her wonderful agent, Caroline. Hennie for the fab artwork, and Sarah for the design. Jennie for the great copy-editing. Tanya, Sophie and Louise for helping Sassy and her friends get out there to the readers. And all the other Puffins who busy away behind the scenes.

Thanks too to Ian, Cathy, Hazel, Keira and Stuart for their invaluable input –
and their inspiration!

Seriously Sassy

Pinch me, I'm dreaming

Maggi Gibson

PUFFIN

To Hazel and Keira
The two brightest stars

PUFFIN BOOKS

Published by the Penguin Group
Penguin Books Ltd, 80 Strand, London WC2R ORL, England
Penguin Group (USA) Inc., 375 Hudson Street, New York, New York 10014, USA
Penguin Group (Canada), 90 Eglinton Avenue East, Suite 700, Toronto, Ontario, Canada M4P 2Y3
(a division of Pearson Penguin Canada Inc.)
Penguin Ireland, 25 St Stephen's Green, Dublin 2, Ireland (a division of Penguin Books Ltd)
Penguin Group (Australia), 250 Camberwell Road, Camberwell, Victoria 3124, Australia
(a division of Pearson Australia Group Pty Ltd)
Penguin Books India Pvt Ltd, 11 Community Centre, Panchsheel Park, New Delhi – 110 017, India
Penguin Group (NZ), 67 Apollo Drive, Rosedale, North Shore 0632, New Zealand
(a division of Pearson New Zealand Ltd)
Penguin Books (South Africa) (Pty) Ltd, 24 Sturdee Avenue, Rosebank, Johannesburg 2196, South Africa

Penguin Books Ltd, Registered Offices: 80 Strand, London WC2R ORL, England

puffinbooks.com

First published 2009
1

Copyright © Maggi Gibson, 2009
All rights reserved

The moral right of the author has been asserted

Set in 13/16 pt Monotype Baskerville by
Palimpsest Book Production Limited, Grangemouth, Stirlingshire
Made and printed in England by Clays Ltd, St Ives plc

British Library Cataloguing in Publication Data
A CIP catalogue record for this book is available from the British Library

ISBN: 978-0-141-32465-4

www.greenpenguin.co.uk

IF YOU WERE A PANDA

If you were a panda
All cuddly, cute and sweet
I'm sure that I'd love you
And when you say 'Let's meet'
I'd jump at the chance
I'd sing and I'd dance
I'd high-five my mates
I'd say I just can't wait
For our very first date . . .

But the thing is this
You're just a guy
When you say hello
I wanna say goodbye.

If you were a polar bear
All fluffy and white
I'm sure I would love you
And when you say 'Tonight?'
I'd jump at the chance
I'd sing and I'd dance
I'd leap in the air
Spend hours doin' my hair.

But the thing is this
You're just a guy

When you say hello
I wanna say goodbye.

If you were a dolphin or a tiny baby seal
I know what I'd think, I know what I'd feel
My heart would melt,
I'd jump up and down for joy.

But the thing is this — you're just a boy
You're not that cuddly, you're not that sweet,
You're not a rare species or under threat
But hey there, chico — don't look so upset
Cos I'm not sayin' never —
I'm only sayin' — not yet!

By Sassy Wilde

Dad's going to kill Pip. That's my little sister. Nine years old at the moment, and unless she finds Houdini, her new Dwarf Hairy-Footed Hamster, and locks him up securely out of Dad's way, she ain't gonna make her tenth birthday. Which means I'm going to end up an only child with a murderer for a father, trailing to visit him in prison with sad little food parcels and the same message every time, *No, Dad, Mum hasn't forgiven you yet.*

Right at this moment Mum's in a bit of a tizz cos there's a photographer and journalist coming to do a piece on Dad – you know the kind of thing, the new MP at home – so me and my bezzies are lying low in my room.

'For goodness' sake, Pip!' Mum howls as she rushes along the landing in her dressing gown, her face plastered with cucumber ten-years-younger mudpack. 'Where did you last see him?'

My best friend, Taslima, is sitting cross-legged on my rainbow rug, scribbling into her new pink notebook. Taslima wants to be a psychologist and she's using my family as her first case study. Basically, she thinks we're all nuts. And sometimes I have to agree. I mean, how's Dad going to cope with the demands of running the country now he's an MP? He can't even run our house.

Take, for example, the loo. It doesn't work properly. It's SO embarrassing. You have to flush *at least* three times to get the most pitiful trickle of water.

Suddenly there's a piercing scream. Taslima looks up from her notebook and we both look towards the door. The toilet flushes (three times) and Cordelia rushes in, followed closely by a hysterically wailing Pip.

Moments later Mum appears.

'Calm down, Pip,' she remonstrates through gritted teeth. Her mudpack's almost dry and she's trying not to crack it. 'The girls will help you find Houdini before Digby gets back.' She flashes us a please-help-me-out-here smile. Big mistake. Her face splits like something from a late-night horror movie.

'Gets back from where?' I ask, putting my guitar down. I had been hoping to let Cordelia and Taslima hear the new song I wrote last night, 'If You Were a Panda'. I wrote the lyrics a while back – before I met Twig, natch – and I've finally worked out some chords and a melody.

'Dad's sent Digby to get a mousetrap.' Pip throws herself on to my bed, her tiny body shuddering with big tragic sobs. 'They're going to kill Houdini! Murder him. In cold blood! And he's only a teensy helpless hamster. Sassy, you've got to do something,' she splutters through a tsunami of tears.

'Calm down, Pip!' Taslima says in an authoritative voice. 'Tell us where his hideouts are, and by a simple process of elimination we'll track him down.'

Amazingly, Pip quietens as if someone's just thrown her 'off' switch.

'Thanks, girls,' Mum sighs. 'I'll go and get this stuff off my face.'

And with that she disappears.

We bundle downstairs to check the places where Houdini's been found on previous escapes. Last time he was in Brewster's dog bowl. Poor old Brewster! He's almost blind and he's not used to sticking his nose into his bowl and his food suddenly moving.

The time before, Houdini was in the rubbish bin under the sink. He tumbled on to Digby's foot with a ribbon of carrot peel dangling from his mouth. Digby thought he was a mouse, jumped up on to the worktop and – can you believe it – screamed the house down!

In the living room Dad's busy flicking through a big pile of papers. I heave the sofa out from the wall. Taslima and Pip peer under the armchairs.

Dad's not helpful in the least. He just witters on about how a wild rodent running amok during his 'New MP at Home' interview is not going to do his public image any good.

'If you don't find him before the newspaper people get here,' he says, putting his papers down, 'I'll have no option but to put a big piece of cheese in a mousetrap and let nature runs its course.'

'Dad!' I protest. 'Mousetraps are NOT natural. Plants are natural. Trees are natural. Mousetraps are man-made. And Houdini doesn't even eat cheese! He's vegan.'

Just then Cordelia comes drifting in, her green eyes shining, which usually means she's communing with some higher level of consciousness.

'Sshhhh . . .' Cordelia says as she stares like a fortune-teller into the depths of Houdini's clear plastic exercise ball. 'I need you to focus your psychic energy in this direction,' she commands.

We all stare at Cordelia – even Dad – as she moans and sways gently, her long black hair falling forward over her face.

'Can you see anything?' I whisper.

'It's . . . small . . . curled up . . . sleeping . . .' Cordelia mutters.

'Where?' Pip breathes.

'Somewhere dark –'

Just then the doorbell rings and Cordelia's eyes snap open.

'That'll be the people from the paper!' Dad gasps. 'They're early.'

Mum takes control. 'OK, everyone. Forget about the hamster. With some luck he'll stay asleep till they've gone.'

Dad pushes the sofa straight, plumps up a couple of cushions and strides off to answer the door. Mum ushers us all out of the living room and gives us strict instructions to stay upstairs and be quiet.

'Sorry, Pip,' Cordelia says as we straggle out. 'I don't think he's far away. And I'm sure he's safe.'

Dad swings the front door wide open with a big welcome-to-the-new-MP's-house flourish.

'Oh, it's you!' he exclaims rudely, and my heart skips a beat. Cos it's not the newspaper people after all. It's Twig!

'Why didn't you come in my bedroom window, like you usually do?' I ask as we all crowd into my room.

'Because there was no one inside to open it?' Twig smiles his lopsided smile.

'We were all downstairs looking for Houdini,' Pip sniffs, her face still tearstained and blotchy. 'Dad's going to kill him if we don't find him.'

'Really?' Twig asks.

Cordelia sinks into my beanbag, exhausted from her psychic efforts, and Pip goes off to search the airing cupboard.

I leap on to the bed and tuck one leg under the other. 'Dad's just a bit tense –'

'Shhh . . .' Twig interrupts, dropping to his knees.

Taslima looks at me, her face a question mark. I shrug. I've only known Twig a few weeks, and OK, I do wear his friendship bracelet – but why he's now got his bottom in the air and his head under my bed, I cannot explain.

'Maybe it's a courtship ritual kind of thing?' Taslima whispers.

'Yeah,' Cordelia mutters. 'Or maybe he's a nut!' And she crosses her eyes and sticks out her tongue.

Suddenly Twig struggles to his feet. Clutching one of my bras! The really pretty lemon one I haven't seen in weeks.

Cordelia's and Taslima's eyes grow wide as satellite dishes. And I'm about to blurt *It's-not-mine-I've-never-seen-it-before-must-be-someone-else's* when I see, snuggled up in one of the cups, sound asleep, something hairy-footed and hamster-shaped![1]

'Pip!' I yell. 'Come and see what Twig's got!'

Seconds later Pip whooshes into the room, takes one glance at the sleeping hamster, throws herself on Twig and covers him in big mwah-mwah kisses.

---

[1] I did say he was a Dwarf Hamster, didn't I? 28A to be precise . . .

As Pip detaches herself Twig catches my eye, and we exchange a look that sends shivers all through me. Quietly, Taslima takes out her pen and scribbles something in her notebook.

'OK, Pip,' I say, my voice high-pitched as a hairy-footed hamster's. 'Put Houdini back in his cage. And make sure it's properly locked this time. Now, anyone want some juice?'

Seconds later I escape downstairs to get some lemonade and try to regain my composure. I'm just coming out of the kitchen with five glasses on a tray when the front doorbell rings. Digby, Dad's personal assistant, has returned with the mousetrap.

He's hardly inside the door when Pip leans over the banister. 'Too late!' she screams. 'Twig found my hamster! You can take your stinky old mousetrap back to the shop. *Murderer!*'

'Pip!' Dad bellows. 'The mousetrap catches the mouse alive. I am NOT a murderer!'

'Can I quote you on that?' says a smart-looking woman who's just followed Digby through the open door.

Dad turns, spluttering, to greet the journalist.

'Welcome to the Wilde Household,' I smile sweetly as I squeeze past. 'You'll be quite safe. Honest.'

2

Taslima and Cordelia have both gone now. Taslima couldn't wait, apparently, to clean out her goldfish tank, while Cordelia just had to go home and babysit her Mum's pet bat.

'Call us later!' Taslima giggled as she made her way up the front path.

'Yeah, we'll get ALL the goss then!' Cordelia smiled mischievously.

As I pass the mirror at the foot of the stairs I check my teeth for bits of stray spinach[2] – or anything else that might make me unkissable. Then I stick my head round Pip's door and warn her – on pain of a slow and tortuous death – NOT to come anywhere near my room. Finally, I head into my own room and close the door firmly.

Twig's standing by the window, gazing out into the leaves of the big old tree. When he turns round and smiles, my heart soars like it's going to fly right up out of the top of my head.

[2] Vegetarian's nightmare.

'Have you got a computer?' he asks.

My heart falters mid-soar. A computer! I had kinda hoped he would say, *why don't you play guitar while I listen adoringly* . . .

'There's only Dad's.' I sigh, wondering if I've got Twig all wrong. 'It's prehistoric. There's no decent games or anything.'

'Great,' Twig says. 'There's something I want to show you. Do you have the Internet?'

'Yeah,' I nod. My heart flutters helplessly in a downward spiral. I mean, if he's just going to play computer all afternoon, I'd be as well helping Taslima clean her goldfish bowl!

As we traipse downstairs to Dad's study – which isn't really a study at all, just a converted cupboard – there's a delicious smell wafting from the kitchen. I guess Mum's baking her extra special home-made gingerbread to prove to the journalist she's a good mother and we're a normal family.

Twig grins up at me as we wait for Dad's computer to whirr into life.

'Aren't you going to sit down?' He shifts along the old piano stool we use as a seat. 'There's plenty of room.'

'I'm OK here, honest!' I insist, standing by the door. 'You won't be long, will you?'

'Got it!' he says suddenly. 'How do you put the volume up?'

But I don't answer. I can't. I'm staring at the

screen. Flabbergasted. Stunned. Because it's me. At the Bluebell Wood protest. Playing guitar and singing!

'The volume?' Twig asks again. I show him the key and he presses until the volume chirrups into action. My voice croaks out of the tinny little speakers and Twig starts to laugh.

'Oh no! I don't really sound like that, do I?' I gasp.

Twig shakes his head. 'Nah! It sounds great on my computer. Brilliant, in fact.'

'But how did it get on the Internet? I mean – who filmed it?'

'Dunno. But somebody did. And look! It's had 569 hits and it's only been up for a few days . . . Oh, 570!' Twig says with a grin.

This little smile spreads across my face. Becomes bigger and bigger until it's not just a smile any longer. It's a big surge of happiness and it comes whooping out of my mouth and I start dancing around. I am so excited! And Brewster starts barking and Pip leans over the stairs and bellows, 'Will you keep quiet, you're going to wake Houdini!' And Mum appears and she's going *Shush-Shush-Shush* and then Dad's there and the journalist and the photographer and they're all saying, *What is it? What's going on?* And Twig shows them the video clip and the journalist says, *WOW! That is so fantastic!* Then Twig points out that the number of hits has gone up by another three!

'Maybe we could take some photos of you with your guitar?' the photographer suggests, changing the lens on his camera.

'That would be so good for the piece. Give an added human-interest angle.' The journalist flicks on her mini-recorder and pushes it into Dad's face. 'So how do you feel about your daughter's ambitions to be a star?'

Poor Dad! I know it's the last thing he wants. He's been boring us for days now with all the serious issues he needs to discuss. You know, the Health Service, Fuel Prices, the Plumbing Problems in Strathcarron High School.

While Dad struggles to turn the interview back on track, Twig runs upstairs to get my guitar. The photographer wants to take the shots out in the garden, seeing as I'm so into green issues.

'Ignore the camera,' the photographer says as I pose in front of a lilac bush. 'Yeah, that's great.'

He's clicking away, and I'm turning my head this way and that, when Pip appears beside me in a long pink dress that makes her look like a walking wedding cake.

'I'd like some shots now on that old swing at the bottom of the garden,' the photographer says.

'Pip's been chosen to be the Sleeping Beauty in her school play,' I explain quietly as I follow him. 'She doesn't always dress like that.'

Then I perch on the swing and strum my guitar. As the photographer clicks, Pip floats across in front of me like she's chasing an invisible butterfly.

'OK,' the photographer sighs. 'That'll be fine. I'll take some of your mum and dad inside now.' And he goes off towards the house, Pip dancing in his wake.

Twig sits cross-legged on the grass and gazes up at me, a strange look on his face.

'What?' I ask, my colour rising.

He hesitates, as if weighing up whether or not to say what's on his mind.

'I was just wondering . . .' he begins.

'Wondering what?'

'If it'll change you.'

'If what'll change me?'

'Getting famous. Being a star.' He squints at me through his fall of hair.

'It's just a clip on the Internet!' I laugh, clipping a capo on to the neck of my guitar. 'It's great (strum) and obviously there's going to be a bit in the paper now (strum), which is fantastic (strum), but it's not like I've got a recording contract or anything (strumstrumstrum).'

Twig's still gazing at me. His eyes are a soft golden brown, and for a split second I imagine him coming over to me, lifting the guitar from my lap . . .

'Anyway,' I continue, snapping myself back to

reality with a noisy twang. 'I don't see why I have to change.'

'Success always changes people,' Twig says. 'Look what happened to Arizona Kelly. She got her first hit at fourteen, and now she's a complete mess, all mixed up in drugs and stuff.'

Arizona Kelly's latest video flashes into my head. Half-naked in a leopard-skin bikini, writhing on the floor with a python, pouting at the camera. Sad enough, but the song was awful too.

'No way will that happen to me!' I exclaim. 'I sing cos I care about things. Like the planet, and animals, and what we're doing to the world. I sing cos I've got something to say. I'm not gonna change just to be famous!'

'So what if they asked you to do a world tour and it was going to cause tons of pollution, and they said if you didn't do it they wouldn't put your albums out?'

I roll my eyes. 'Twig! As if I'm going to do a world tour!'

'But isn't that what you want?'

'I suppose so,' I say slowly. 'But it's not going to happen . . . And even if it did, I know what I will and won't do. I really, honestly, absolutely am not going to change.'

'Really?' Twig asks.

'Really,' I answer. And I mean it.

Totally.

3

Sunday night.

Earlier, when everyone else was out, I watched this documentary on TV, all about little kids working in sweatshops in Third World countries, making clothes to be sold in the UK. It was really shocking. So now I'm in my room, trying to write a song about how I feel, but I must have some sort of block on my creativity cos I can't make anything come at all.

Finally I give in and practise some chords instead. Then I get ready for bed and tuck up under the covers with Little Ted. But I can't get to sleep. Cos my head starts to spin with all these things to worry about. Little kids slaving in sweatshops; bottle-nosed dolphins and hammerhead turtles and red-ruffed lemurs facing extinction. And famines; and earthquakes; and floods; and Agnes my Adopted Donkey in the Dorset Donkey Sanctuary. I mean, just where am I going to get the fiver a month I've pledged to keep her in

Donkey Luxury until she goes to the Big Donkey Retreat in the sky?

My brain spins and whirrs like a frisbee in a whirlwind. Finally I sit up and click the bedside lamp on. When I was teensy and having a bad dream Mum used to make me get out of bed and go to the loo and brush my teeth, then she'd tuck me back under the covers like I was going to bed for the first time. So that's what I do. I get up and brush my teeth, then climb back into bed again and put the lamp off. This time, as I close my eyes, I make myself think of all the good things in the world. All the lovely things . . .

Dad says the piece the journalist and photographer did yesterday will be in Tuesday's paper. I'm so excited. I mean, that's how you get a breakthrough, isn't it? You have a clip on the Internet, then a piece in the paper, and before you know it there's someone offering you a recording contract, and hey presto! You have everything you ever wished for.

But what if Twig's right? What if I sign a recording contract, then they want me to do things I don't want to do?

I click the bedside lamp back on and pull my TOTALLY SECRET NOTEBOOK from my bedside drawer. I flick it open and write at the top of a clean page.

THINGS I WILL NEVER DO JUST TO BE A STAR
I, Sassy Wilde, aged 13, do formally swear that I will
never do any of the following:

1. Wear fur or do anything involving cruelty to
   animals.
2. Travel in non-environmentally friendly ways.
3. Kiss anyone on video (unless it's T**6).
4. Wear stupid clothes that make me look
   cheap and nasty.
5. Strip off. My body is private property and
   it's gonna stay that way!
6. Let any of my albums be made by poor
   people in Third World countries who aren't
   getting paid properly.
7. Take drugs of any kind. Ever.
8. Do adverts for anything 'cept things like
   Friends of the Forest, Friends of the Fowl,
   Friends of the Earth, Save the Planet, Save
   the Children, Save the Stick Insects, and
   Greenpeace.
9. Change anything in my songs because
   someone else wants me to.
10. Most of all I will never, ever forget that
    Cordelia and Taslima are my soul sisters
    and best buds forever.

There. I think I've just about covered everything.
I feel much happier now.

I can't control the whole world. But I can control the little bit of it that's Sassy Wilde. I've struck a bargain with myself. I should be able to keep it, shouldn't I?

I switch the lamp off once more. And at last fall into a deep and dreamless sleep.

4

School this morning's a bit weird!

In IT, Megan – that's Twig's stepsis and my ex-bezzie – tells Midge Murphy about the video clip of me on the Internet.

And Midge Murphy tells our IT teacher, Mrs Smith, and Mrs Smith insists on downloading it so the whole class can watch.

'So who filmed it?' Mrs Smith asks, once we've played it for the third time and Midge has had great fun starting and stopping and running it backwards so I look and sound like a halfwit.

'Maybe it was that new kid, Twig!' Sindi-Sue says excitedly. 'You know, the weird guy.'

'Hey!' Megan exclaims fiercely. 'That's my stepbro you're talking about.'

'It couldn't have been him, stupid!' Magnus Menzies points at the screen. 'See! He's up in the tree beside Sassy!'

I fire Magnus a filthy look, but he totally misunderstands and smiles back, all friendly-like.

Honestly, Magnus may be swim-champ, he may have a brain the size of Belgium, but he's got the emotional intelligence of a shrivelled peanut. What's more, Magnus and me have history. Bad history.

'I've got a hunch.' Cordelia spreads her black-nailed fingers wide. 'Of course, I don't have any evidence. But my gut feeling is . . .' She pauses for dramatic effect. 'It was Miss Cassidy.'

'Miss Cassidy?' Magnus scoffs. 'Our art teacher?'

'Well, she was in a tree just opposite Sassy,' Midge Murphy says. 'So if she's got one of them mobiles with a video-thingie on it, she could've done it well-easy.'

'But listen to the sound quality.' Mrs Smith turns the volume up. 'You wouldn't get that kind of recording on a mobile. No, this has been done on a camcorder. And a good one at that.'

'It doesn't really matter,' I shrug. 'Though I *would* like to know who did it – so I could thank them.'

'Well, whoever it is must really like you,' Mrs Smith says, and Magnus grins at me. 'Because if you want to make it as a singer, Sassy, you need publicity. This is a great start.'

'And that's not all that's happening, Miss!' Megan blurts excitedly. 'Twig says Sassy's photo's gonna be in the paper tomorrow.'

'They might not put it in, Megan!' I gasp. 'I really didn't want anyone to know!'

'Sorreee!' Megan trills and her colour rises. 'Twig should've said if I wasn't to tell anyone!'

'A piece in the paper! That's so exciting,' Mrs Smith beams, ignoring the prickly vibes. 'You'll soon not want to know any of us, you'll be so rich and famous!'

'But I don't want to be rich and famous! I just want people to hear my songs. I'll always be the same old Sassy. I'll still have the same friends.' I smile at Taslima and Cordelia.

'Yeah,' says Megan, putting her arm round my shoulder. 'And we'll always be there for you, Sass.'

I shrink away from Megan's arm. The thing is, we had this big fall-out at the end of P7 – cos she stole something from me and lied about it and got me into BIG trouble. Even though it was a long time ago and she kinda made up with me recently, I'm still not sure I can trust her. And I'm not sure I want her as one of my buds.

Well, not one of my close buds anyway.

The following morning when I go yawning down for breakfast, Mum's bouncing about the kitchen like a kid high on E-numbers. Which is *not* normal. Mum is not a morning person. Usually Dad has to do everything while Mum bumbles about in her dressing gown, bumping into furniture and making low groaning noises like a hippo with indigestion.

I'm just getting some kiwi and banana together

for a smoothie when Pip breezes in and pops Houdini on the table. He immediately scampers over to the breakfast toast and starts nibbling.

'Mu-u-um!' I squeal. 'Are you going to let her do that? It's s-o-o-o unhygienic.'

'No, it's not,' Pip pipes up primly. 'Houdini keeps himself very clean. In fact, he washes first thing every morning. Anyway he's hungry. And he's part of the family. Just as much as you are.'

I roll my eyes heavenward. Until a couple of weeks ago Pip looked – and acted – like a crazy Lolitaz Doll. Now she's gone all nature-friendly, and OK, it's a big improvement, but no way am I sharing my breakfast with a Dwarf Hairy-Footed Hamster!

Houdini gives me a filthy look, then scutters across the table – leaving a trail of hamster poo.

'Mu-u-u-u-u-m!' I wail, horrified.

'OK! OK!' Mum intervenes. 'Houdini can go in here, Pip.' And she plops a glass baking bowl on the table and scoops Houdini into it. 'There,' she says, sticking a lettuce leaf in with him. 'He can stay at table with us. OK, Sassy? And you, Pip, can disinfect the table!'

Just then there's a thud in the hall as the morning paper drops through the door. Brewster starts barking. (He lies right under the letter box even though the paper lands on him every morning.) Pip squeals excitedly and runs to get it.

Seconds later she reappears, trying to find the page with the bit about Dad. But the whole thing comes apart in her hands. Brewster, still over-excited, comes storming in, barking wildly, and tramples all over the fallen paper. Pip bursts into tears of frustration. Mum and I scramble on the floor, trying to salvage the page with Dad's feature.

'For goodness' sake!' Dad splutters as he comes into the kitchen and finds Mum and me on our knees and Pip sniffling. 'What on earth's going on here?'

Mum blinks up at him. 'Paper's arrived, darling,' she smiles, just as I grab the page, *The New MP at Home*, and smooth it out on the floor, a trillion nervous bats twitching in my tummy.

'What a brilliant photo!' Mum exclaims, taking it from me and putting it on the table where all of us can see.

And it is. A really brilliant photo. Of Mum and Dad and Pip in her big pink dress.

But there's no photo of me. Not even a tiny one.

'Oh, Sass, I'm so sorry,' Dad says, ruffling my hair. 'That's the thing with newspapers. You're never sure what they'll put in and what they'll leave out.'

'No sweat, Dad. It wasn't meant to be about me anyway,' I smile bravely, trying to hide my disappointment. 'Anyway, you look gorgeous,' I say to Pip as she squeezes between me and Mum to see the photo.

'Aaawwwww, Pip,' Mum coos. 'You are *so* photogenic.'

'Which is why I'd like to be a model.' Pip flashes Mum a smile. 'But an environmentally aware one.'

'Are you OK, Sass?' Mum asks as I quietly head for the door. 'You're not too upset about not being in the paper?'

And that's when I see it. Staring back at me from a crumpled page on the floor.

I tug it from under Brewster's paws and smooth it out.

'Wowww!' Pip squeals as she sees the headline. 'That is so-o-o-o cool, Sassy! You got a whole piece to yourself!'

I stare in bewilderment.

SALLY WILDE SINGS TO SAVE THE PLANET

Hamster-mad Sally, aged 9, has always wanted to be a supermodel. But this sweet little songbird's got more than one talent.

With a clip on the Internet fast getting hits, who knows how far she might go. 'My big dream's to be the next Arizona Kelly,' Sally told our reporter in her childish lisp.

And with looks like that, we tip this youngster for the top!

Check her out on www.seeme.com/sassywildesings

'Oh dear,' Mum says, reading over my shoulder.

'I would NEVER say I want to be like Arizona Kelly!' I splutter.

'That's the thing with journalists. They can't be trusted,' Dad sighs. 'They make up things you never said.'

'But ARIZONA KELLY!!!'

'What's wrong with Arizona Kelly?' Pip pipes up. 'I like Arizona Kelly!'

'Well, I don't,' I fume. 'And I'm not hamster-mad. And I'm not nine. And my name's not Sally! And I don't lisp! They have got me totally muddled up with you, Pip!'

'But apart from that, it's fine, isn't it?" Mum says hopefully. 'And it *is* a lovely photo.'

'And look, they've got the weblink right,' Dad adds brightly. 'Must have been the spellchecker changed Sassy to Sally in the main piece.'

Trailing my heart behind me like a dead fish, I plod upstairs to get my ruckie. The newspaper's portrayed me as a nine-year-old empty airhead[3]. If anyone at school gets hold of it I will be relentlessly teased.

In my room I text Cordelia and Taslima.

SOS!!! EMRGNCY!!!! MT @ FD ASAP! Sx

[3] Taslima says: if there's air in the head is it actually empty?

Just then the grandfather clock in the hall chimes nine. Which it isn't. Mum sets it half an hour fast so we'll never be late for anything. I take a deep breath, thunder downstairs, whizz out of the house and make for the Fire Door round the back of the school to wait for my bezzies to come and save me from disaster.

'Calm down!' Taslima soothes as I explain the tragic turn of events. 'No one reads that awful paper anyway.'

'She's right,' says Cordelia, yawning sleepily. 'Just keep quiet about it. There's really no need for anyone to know.'

'Yeah, but Megan only went and told everyone there would be a bit in the paper,' I groan.

'But Megan didn't say WHICH paper,' Taslima reasons. 'There's tons of different ones. Nobody's going to look through them just to find a bit about you, are they?'

Just then the second bell rings. It's nine o'clock. We should be in class by now.

'You're worrying about the wrong thing, Sass,' Taslima says as she swings her ruckie on to her shoulder. 'What you *should* be worrying about is whether or not we can get from here to Registration without Mr Smollett spotting us and giving us detention.'

I think I am the luckiest girl on earth to have

two bezzies like Cordelia and Taslima. I fly into such a panic sometimes, but Taslima can always calm me down and make me see things aren't so bad. *A problem*, Taslima says, *is just a challenge waiting for a solution.* Cordelia, on the other hand, is the person you want on your side if you need protection. A quick flash from her green eyes sees off most pests.

We arrive breathlessly at Miss Peabody's Registration class, but the door is closed. Not a good sign.

'Let me do the talking,' Cordelia whispers. Taslima and I nod our agreement. Because she writes the most amazingly imaginative stories,[4] Miss Peabody thinks Cordelia is wonderful.

Cordelia opens the door and we follow her in. She's just about to charm the handknitted socks off Miss Peabody when Midge Murphy shouts, 'Give us a smile, Arizona Sally!' Then he dives about making a camera shape with his hands and clicking furiously. Everyone's laughing and the boys are whistling and my face is burning.

'OK, girls,' Miss Peabody sighs. 'Just go to your

[4] In fact, Cordelia simply writes about her life at home. Miss Peabody just THINKS Cordelia makes it all up! I mean, how many people really have a pet bat and a mum who's a witch?

seats. It's really too early in the morning for all this celebrity stuff.'

Can you believe it? In history, last period this afternoon, Magnus Menzies passed me a note – asking me out! Apparently he thinks the piece in the paper is great. Any publicity is good publicity, he says. And as he was voted Most Desirable Boy in S1,[5] he thinks we'd make a 'hot couple'. But I have already been out with Magnus Menzies. I was young and naive and it all ended badly. My deep emotional scars are still healing and I have no desire to re-open them. The boy must be a raving lunatic if he thinks I would ever go out with him again!

In fact I was scribbling all that down, describing in detail why he is the person I am least likely to go out with EVER – coming last after:

1. Smelly Smollett
2. Osama Bin Laden
3. Mr Bean

when, tragically, the bell rang and I didn't get the chance to pass it to him.

Cordelia, Taslima and me link arms as we spill

[5] I voted for Midge Murphy. A sympathy vote, really. No one else was going to.

out of school, and guess what? Everyone seems to have completely forgotten about the piece in the paper!

'That's because,' Taslima explains as we head for the bus stop, 'the average person has a three-second attention span. Already, Sassy, you are old news.'

We're going straight from school to the shops so Taslima can spend the dosh her great-gran sent last week from Pakistan. 'I want some new clothes and stuff,' she'd said yesterday in biology. 'And I'd love to treat you both to a giant milkshake!'

The thought of that milkshake has kept me going through a double of maths, an excruciating period of English and an eternity of history.

At the bus stop there's already a long straggling queue. Just as we tag on at the end, Megan spots us and comes rushing over. She starts chatting to Taslima and Cordelia, and I let them get on with it.

On the other side of the road Magnus and Beano Bartlett are fooling about, whacking each other with their jackets, hooting loudly, obviously trying to get our attention. And I'm wondering whether I should rummage in my bag for the note I wrote in English and run across and shove it into Magnus's hand . . . when who comes whizzing along on his BMX, but Twig!

'Hi, Sass!' he says breathlessly as he jumps off and lands beside me.

There's something about Twig. When I see him it's like the sun has come out on a cloudy day.

'I thought we could maybe go to your place?' Twig half says, half asks. 'I've brought my dad's camcorder.' He turns so I can see the ruckie on his back.

'Whoa, stepbro!' Megan butts in. 'Your dad will kill you if he finds out! You'd better take it home right away!'

Pointedly, Twig ignores her. 'I thought I could make another video of you singing. Put it online for your fans.'

Magnus has stopped fooling around and I know he's watching, trying to hear what we're saying. And I so want to go with Twig and not turn him down, especially as it would be such a sickener for Magnus, but it's not right to run out on your girl-buds just cos a chico turns up, is it?

All these thoughts are whizzing through my brain like an express train through an empty station, when Cordelia exclaims, 'You should go with Twig, Sass! Make another video. You've gotta use things like that if you're gonna get anywhere. I'll make sure Tas finds something absolutely sprodulious!'[6]

'Cordelia's right, Sassy. You should go with Twig,' Taslima smiles. 'That is, if you want to. I

[6] Special & super & beautiful & gorgeous.

don't mind. Honest. We can have that giant milkshake another time.'

I look from Cordelia to Taslima. They have to be the best bezzie buds ever. Then I notice Magnus glowering at Twig, and I know it's not nice of me to want to hurt him – but his ego could do with a bit of deflating. And what I'm about to do is a lot more eloquent than the big long ranting note I wrote in English.

'OK, Twig. That would be great,' I say, then I hug the two best bezzies ever, wave a friendly bye-ee to Megan, and wander off down the road with Twig.

5

On the way home I tell Twig all about the horrendous bit in the paper.

'I know. I saw it earlier,' Twig says, balancing on the pedals of the BMX as he waits for me to catch up. 'But maybe it's good it happened. You know now not to trust journalists and photographers –'

'Aren't you about to photograph me?' I interrupt mischievously.

'That's different,' Twig grins. 'I'm on your side, remember?'

And when he says that I get this warm feeling. I like having Twig on my side. And I trust him totally. I know he'll film me the way I would want.

I've still got that warm feeling and we're chatting away about nothing and everything, when we turn into our road and my jaw drops open in horror. Parked in the driveway of my house there's this great huge black four-wheel drive monstrosity – you know the kind that contributes MASSIVELY to global warming.

'So whose is *that*?' Twig asks as Brewster comes bumbling towards us, blindly sniffing the air.

'Digby said some bigwig politician was coming to visit Dad. To discuss green issues, would you believe?'

'Sheesh!' Twig snorts as he heaves his BMX over the hedge and drops it on to the front lawn. 'No wonder the world's in such a mess.'

'Personally,' I say, squeezing past the huge machine that's all but blocking the path to the front door, 'I can't stand people who drive those things. They should be found guilty of Crimes against the Planet and be made to do, like a zillion hours Community Service –'

'I'd send them to Boot Camp,' Twig grins. 'BOOT CAMP FOR ECO BADDIES. Hard-labour planting trees to offset all the carbon dioxide their silly Hummers are pumping out into the atmosphere.'

In the hallway I shout, 'I'm home!' like I always do, and chuck my ruckie in the general direction of the coat stand. Through the glass door to the kitchen we see a man and a woman sitting at the pine table. Mum's serving them coffee and home-made muffins, and I'm about to slip upstairs with Twig when Mum waves frantically through the glass.

Twig and me exchange a glance. 'Looks like I've got to go in and do the perfect daughter act for Dad's visitors,' I mutter.

'See you in a minute,' says Twig. 'I'll set up the camcorder.' And he disappears up to my room.

As I open the kitchen door, Mum leaps to her feet and beams at me. 'This,' she exclaims excitedly, 'is Sassy!'

The man and woman stare, like I'm some kind of freak. I keep my scowl firmly in place. I don't care if they are Very Important People. As Major Polluters of the Planet they are not getting a smile out of me! Unfortunately they don't seem to register my disapproval. Which infuriates me further.

'Can I go now, Mum?' I ask sulkily.

'Sassy!' the man says in a friendly voice. I sigh heavily and roll my eyes heavenwards. 'Your mum was just telling us how passionate you are about all things environmental. That's great. She says you want to save the planet.'

I really don't know how to explain what happens next. One minute I'm thinking how desperate I am to get back to Twig, the next I'm ranting like I've got no control over my tongue. 'And I take it you're the owner of that dirty great gas guzzler blocking the drive,' I hear myself saying. 'Don't you know that driving a HUMMER in town causes like three times as much pollution as an ordinary car?'

The words come rolling out, the way sometimes the loo roll starts spinning and before you know it there's miles and miles of it on the floor . . .

'I mean, what chance does the planet have if people like *you* can't even choose green vehicles?'

'Sassy!' Mum splutters through a mouthful of muffin, spraying crumbs everywhere.

The cool-looking woman frowns as she delicately picks some of Mum's stray muffin from her low-cut top. She looks incredibly tanned, as if she flies off every weekend to somewhere hot and sunny. And I'm about to tell her about the ghastly polluting effects of short-haul flights when she says something I don't understand at all.

'So it does what it says on the tin.'

By this point I'm standing in a little puddle of my own sweat, wondering if it's deep enough yet to drown myself. Thousands of thoughts are rushing through my brain at once. The biggest being: *Oh no. Dad's going to kill me.* The next biggest: *Why do I always have to say what I'm thinking?*

I'm so upset that I've probably ruined my dad's brand-new political career I don't realize right away that both the man and woman are smiling.

'She's everything we hoped for,' the man says to Mum.

Then the woman stands up and holds her hand out for me to shake. 'Zing. Zing Williams. I'm very pleased to meet you, Sassy.'

'And I'm Ben,' the man says. 'Talent spotter for Y-Gen Music. We saw the piece in yesterday's paper, checked out your video clip on the Internet –'

'Did I just hear right?' I blurt. 'You're from Y-Gen Music? The recording company?'

As Ben and Zing nod in unison, I sink into a chair that Mum pushes under my bottom. I can't believe it. I have dreamed about this moment for so long. I pinch myself cos I think I must be dreaming. And it hurts! Which means this is real. And I'm the happiest girl in the whole entire world!

6

'It's not just about being able to sing,' Zing explains, while Mum brews more coffee. 'After all, there are plenty of girls your age can sing.'

'Sassy writes all her own songs too,' Pip pipes up. Pip came bouncing into the kitchen as soon as she got home from school. She's almost as excited as me.

'That's a huge plus. That's what makes you so distinctive, Sassy. It means you've got your own style,' says Ben.

'And,' says Zing, 'it's great you're so passionate about the environment. Lots of kids out there feel just like you, like their world's being messed up, but they don't have a way of expressing it.'

'Or making their voices heard. That's what we'd like to help you do, Sassy. Make your voice heard.'

'But we need to get you into a recording studio. Put you through your paces. See if you've got what it takes.'

I'm reeling. It's as if someone's stuck me in the washing machine and set it on fast spin.

'So you want me to go to a recording studio?' I croak.

'Yep,' Ben says, tipping half the sugar bowl into his coffee. 'Just so happens we've got some studio time free, which is quite rare really. So if you can make it, and if it's fine with your mum,' he says, flashing Mum a perfect white-toothed smile, 'we'd like you to come straight to the studio after school this Friday. You can have a full session, let us see what you have to offer, then we'll bring you safely home by ten.'

'Of course,' I say, my heart beating faster than the speed of light. 'Yeah. Fine. I mean, that all sounds great!'

Mum takes a deep breath. 'I'm not sure, honey. You're only thirteen . . .'

'You're welcome to come too, Mrs Wilde,' Ben smiles.

I look at Mum with big pleading eyes and I can see her soften, and I know she's about to say yes when suddenly Pip lets out a wail. 'But you can't, Mum. It's my play on Friday after school!'

Mum slaps her forehead. 'Course it is, cookie,' she says.

'I've got the lead in *Sleeping Beauty*,' Pip explains to Ben and Zing, fluttering her lashes in mock modesty. 'I'm a very good actress.'

'Oh, I don't know what to do for the best,' Mum says, running her fingers through her hair so it all sticks up on end and makes her look completely mad. 'Maybe Dad and Digby could go to your play, Pip, and I could go with Sassy.'

Pip's face crumbles. 'But I want *you* to be there, Mummy,' she says in a tiny hurt voice. (Pip wasn't kidding when she said she was a very good actress. This is an Oscar-winning performance.)

'I'll be absolutely fine without you, Mum,' I blurt. 'Really. I don't have a problem going on my own. It's not like I'm a kid.'

'We'll take good care of her, Mrs Wilde,' Zing smiles.

'Ple-e-ease, Mum.' I plead. 'You know I'm not going to do anything silly.'

Mum looks from me to Pip and she knows she's beaten.

'OK, Sassy. But I'll need to run it by your father. I know he'll want to check out the company, make sure everything's as it should be. And he won't be home till later.'

'Look, we'll leave our card,' Zing says, standing up and straightening her jacket. She hands Mum a small black business card with a jazzy purple design and silver lettering.

'Phone once you've spoken to your husband, Mrs Wilde.' Ben stands up and takes out his car keys. 'And if Sassy's father's on board, we'll send a car to pick her up after school on Friday.'

At the door Ben turns and fixes me with piercing blue eyes. 'We love what we've heard of your music, Sassy. We've been looking for a teen girl who can really sing for some time, you know, a kind of female Phoenix Macleod. Who knows, you might be the one!'

A female Phoenix Macleod! Wow! Phoenix Macleod has to be one of the coolest singer songwriters around. He even picked up a Brit Award last year, and he's not much older than me.

I stand in the doorway and wave as the big Hummer roars into life and disappears up the road.

And at last my world, which has been spinning crazily since I walked into the kitchen, starts to steady.

7

And that's when I remember Twig!

I rush up to my room two steps at a time. I can't wait to tell him my news!

But the room's empty. The window's open, the curtains fluttering in the breeze. I lean out and shout down to the garden.

There's no answer.

I thunder downstairs again, leap over Brewster who's running in slow arthritic circles in the hallway, and dash out the front door. Twig's BMX is gone.

I dart into the garage, leap on my bike and pedal like fury down the road. Poor Twig! He must have thought I'd forgotten all about him. (Which I had. Ooops!) But when he hears why, he's bound to be as delighted as I am.

Five minutes later I let my bike fall on Twig's lawn and rush up to his front door. I'm so excited that when I press the buzzer I forget to release it.

At last the door opens. 'OK! OK! What's the emergency?'

But it's not Twig. It's Megan.

'Sassy!' she says, her face a picture of confusion. 'Have you finished the video then?'

'It's a long story,' I gasp. 'I need to speak to Twig. Is he here?'

'But he's at yours,' she frowns. And I'm about to launch into an explanation of how he was but he's not any more, when a grinning face appears over her shoulder.

'Hi, Sass! What's up?'

I blink. It's my turn to be confused now. 'I thought you and Tas were at the Mall?' I say to Cordelia.

'Change of plan,' she laughs. 'A while after you left the bus *still* hadn't come, and Magnus and Beano were being really irritating, you know, showing off in that silly hyper way, being utterly *puerile*, and Megan said she had tons of stuff she didn't wear any more that Taslima might like –'

'– and I was only going to give it all to the charity shop anyway,' Megan adds. 'So I thought my bezzies should have first choice.'

Something twangs inside me when Megan calls Taslima and Cordelia her bezzies. Like when a guitar string breaks.

'Come on in!' Cordelia takes my hand and pulls me inside. 'We're all up in Megan's room.'

'Yeah, Sass!' Megan says, suddenly all friendly – but is it just surface-friendly? Cos I'm not sure she's really that pleased to see me. 'You can look through the stuff too. There might be something you'd like!'

Just then Taslima appears on the stairs in a glittery baby-pink top and tight white jeans. 'What do you think?' she asks, twirling round a few times, her hands above her head.

'You look so-o-o-o cool!' Cordelia laughs. 'Now THAT is STYLE!'

'Come on up, Sassy, and see what else I've chosen!' Tas says excitedly, and before I know it I'm halfway up the stairs. I've just gone into Megan's room, which is completely carpeted in clothes, when Cordelia stops suddenly and places a hand on my forehead.

'There's something you're not telling us, Sassy,' she says, her green eyes narrowing. 'So give! What is it?'

I had kinda wanted Twig to be the first to know, but I can't wait forever to tell someone my good news, can I? So seconds later I'm telling them how we went back to my house and there were these people I thought were to do with Dad's work, and how it turned out they were talent-spotters from Y-Gen Music.

'Y-Gen Music!' Cordelia exclaims. 'Wow! They're the best! Didn't they discover Phoenix Macleod?'

'Yeah! They saw the bit in the paper, and then

they watched the video clip online and now they want me to go to their recording studio in Edinburgh on Friday afternoon!'

'But that's brilliant!' Taslima throws her arms round me in a huge hug. 'I am SO happy for you!'

'This calls for a celebration!' Megan bounces twice on the bed, then leaps to the floor. 'Let's have a big fat sundae!'

And that's what we're doing when Twig finds us.

Sitting in the kitchen, pigging out, spluttering choccy ice cream at each other, sticking blobs of scooshy white cream on our noses.

Twig looks startled, like he's just stumbled on a witches' coven. And before I can swallow and say anything, Megan's blurted out my news about the recording people.

Twig listens silently.

And I wait for him to go, *Wow, that's great, Sass,* and high-five me and maybe even hug me, but all he does is stare at Megan as if she's just told him something really boring, like the price of fish or something. Then he turns his back on us, opens the fridge and pours himself a glass of milk. Suddenly the room is totally silent, the atmosphere taut as a tambourine skin.

'Look, Twig, I'm sorry about earlier,' I say quietly.

'So am I,' Twig mutters.

Cordelia and Taslima and Megan sit frozen, spoons suspended in mid-air.

'I came to look for you as soon as I could. I'm sorry. I was just so excited –'

'– that you forgot I existed?' Twig interrupts.

'No!' I gasp. 'That's not fair!'

Twig drains the last of the milk, puts his glass in the sink and noisily rinses it with cold water. Cordelia, Taslima and Megan slip out of the room.

'Look, Twig, I really wanted you to make the video – I still do. I think it's a great idea. I didn't realize I was with the recording people so long. You should have come down to the kitchen to look for me. I just completely forgot –'

'That's the point, Sassy,' he sighs. 'Some flash-looking people turn up in a monstrous four-wheel drive and suddenly you forget everything – and everyone – else.'

'That's not true!' I gasp.

'How's it not true?' he says, spinning round to face me. 'That's exactly what happened. One minute you were saying you hate people who drive huge cars like that, who don't give a damn about anyone but themselves. And next minute, just because they're from a recording company, you think they're great!'

I stare at Twig. I can't believe what he's saying.

'I thought you were different,' he goes on, his voice so quiet I can hardly hear it. 'I thought you cared. But maybe you don't. Not really.' He pauses. 'Maybe you only care about yourself.'

'I suppose you always do the right thing, do you?' I explode. 'So, I forgot you were waiting for me. Because I was excited. I've dreamed about a moment like that for years. Can you imagine what it means to a singer when someone turns up from a record company? And it's not like I've signed with them. I've just agreed to go to the studio and do some run-throughs. See what they might offer . . .'

My voice trails off. Twig stares at his feet. He looks so unhappy. All my anger disappears as suddenly as it blew up.

'Twig, I'm not going to sell out. I know what I will and won't do. I'm not going to betray everything I believe in. And I'm NOT going to forget my friends.'

Twig looks at me long and hard, like he's looking right into my soul.

'Whatever,' he says quietly, and disappears into the garden.

8

The last few days have been awful.

I have heard nothing from Twig. He's not been on the school wall waiting for me at half three. Of course, I've been acting like I don't care, but the truth is, I do. Megan offered to take a note home to him if I wanted, but I said no. I don't want Megan acting as a go-between. What if she read the note? Or showed it to someone else. I just don't think I can trust her. And I'm way too proud to ask her if he's said anything. So I've pretended I couldn't care less. Maybe I'm just never going to meet a chico I really get on with. Maybe I'm just going to be a career girl. Which is absolutely totally completely fine by me.

Every night this week when I asked Dad if he'd checked out the Y-Gen people he said, 'Ooops, sorry, Sass, I've had so much to do, I clean forgot.'

Only when I threatened last night to begin divorce proceedings against him on the grounds that he was an unfit dad, putting the needs of his political career before my needs as a daughter, did I get some action. Finally, today, Dad got Digby to check Y-Gen out. And, wey-hey! And whoop! whoop! whoop! They're completely legal and above board! (Which I knew already or Phoenix Macleod wouldn't be with them, would he?)

So Mum phoned Ben at Y-Gen this afternoon and it's all arranged. They're sending a car to pick me up straight after school tomorrow!

I am totally completely over the moon. And Saturn. And Mars and Venus. And Pluto and Uranus. And several other planets besides. In fact I'm not even sure I'm still in the Milky Way. I wouldn't be at all surprised to find I've slipped through a black hole and entered a parallel universe where dreams come true.

Of course a bit of me is nervous about tomorrow too. I mean, I don't know what to expect. What if my voice suddenly disappears? Or what if all my guitar strings snap at once? What if overnight I go tone deaf and end up sounding like Sindi-Sue doing karaoke or Midge Murphy doing his dying cat impersonation?

'You'll need some make-up in case you're doing a screen test,' Pip says as she shimmies into my room in her little black negligee and stuffs a pink zip-up bag into my ruckie. 'So I've nicked some of Mum's for you.'

'Cheers, Pip,' I say absent-mindedly, packing my guitar into its big old guitar case. As Pip boogies off to feed Houdini, I flump on my beanbag and flick through my song notebooks. I don't know how many songs they'll want to hear, but I've picked out five that are my faves. I finally managed to write the one about kids being forced to work in sweatshops, so I'm going to do it, cos it's something I feel really strongly about.

I sing the lines through in my head.

She slaves every day in a clothes factory
Nine years old and she doesn't get to play
She sews and she stitches from dawn until dusk
To make cheap clothes for people like us
So why do we buy them?
Why don't we care?
Would we feel the same
If we were working there?
Would you turn away
And not want to know
If the kid who was slaving
Was your little sis or bro?

We care about the polar bears,
The penguins and the trees
So why not care about
Sweatshop kids like these?

Sweatshop kid, it shouldn't be this way
While we're having fun
It's you that has to pay
Sweatshop kid, it shouldn't be this way
While we're having fun,
You never get to play . . .

Then I go through to Pip's room where she's all tucked up under her pink satin duvet, waiting for me to read *Princess Popsicle and the Naughty Peanut*. She's far too old for it really, and she's perfectly well able to read herself, but I'm glad she still wants me to do a bedtime story sometimes. It feels sort of safe and cosy.

When I finish she gives me a big hug. 'When you're famous,' she whispers as she snuggles up to me, 'will you still make time to read me bedtime stories?'

'Course I will.' I tuck her in and kiss the top of her head. 'You're my little sis, aren't you? I'll always have time to read you *Princess Popsicle and the Naughty Peanut*.'

'Even when I'm, like really old, like nineteen or something?' she asks sleepily.

'Even when you're really old,' I reassure her. 'Like ninety-nine or something.'

She giggles and snuggles down under the covers so all that's showing is the top of her head. I tiptoe out.

By the time I get back to my own room there's a new text message from Cordelia.

```
Jst cst spll 4 u 4 2moro. Omens gd. Cx
```

I smile as I text Cordelia back. Then, yawning, I climb into bed and pull my duvet up over my ears. I am so lucky. Lucky to be getting a break. Lucky to have friends like Cordelia and Taslima. Lucky, lucky, lucky . . .

So why can't I get to sleep?

Half an hour later I'm still awake. I bash my pillow and kick my duvet off. I try sleeping upside down. I lie with my feet halfway up the wall, with my pillow on top of my head, with my duvet up over my ears, with my duvet on the floor.

But nothing works.

Which is not fair. Because I should be sound asleep having lovely dreams about singing at the Glastonbury festival. Or collecting my first platinum disc.

Downstairs the old grandfather clocks booms out midnight. In desperation, I sit up. There's only one thing for it. A fridge raid.

I creep out on to the landing. From my parents' room I can hear Dad snoring. At least I hope it's Dad. I'd hate to think Mum could snore like that.[7]

---

[7] Let's just say it's like a cross between an elephant with a cold and a constipated crocodile.

There's no sound from Pip's room except for Houdini spinning furiously on his exercise wheel.

I pad downstairs without putting any lights on. Brewster, in his basket in the hall, looks like a ghost dog, eerily white in the shadows. He's chasing imaginary rabbits in his sleep – or maybe it's imaginary lady dogs – his paws twitching furiously.

I tiptoe past him and into the kitchen. As I open the fridge a pool of yellow light floods out. Carefully, I pour a big glass of milk, then take a banana from the fruit bowl. Milk and banana, Taslima says, provide a combination of chemicals that should make you fall asleep easily.

Minutes later I've scoffed the banana and gulped down the milk. But I still don't feel in the least sleepy. I just feel sad. Which doesn't make any sense at all. I'm thirteen years old. I've just had a video on the Internet. I'm getting the chance to impress a brilliant record company. All I've got to do is play my guitar and sing, which I totally love doing . . .

Just then Brewster whimpers and the kitchen door opens. Mum switches the light on and I blink against the sudden brightness.

'What's wrong, sweetie?' she asks, pulling her robe tight around her waist.

'Nothing,' I lie. 'I'm a bit over-excited, that's all. I was just on my way back to bed.'

What I don't say is what's really bothering me.

And what I've spent all week trying not to acknowledge. I upset Twig and I really, really didn't mean to, and I don't know how to explain that to him, and I'm not sure he wants to hear my explanation anyway.

Mum gives me a big hug. 'You know, you don't have to do this recording thing tomorrow,' she whispers into my hair. 'I can phone them in the morning. Say you're not ready for it yet. You're young, Sassy. You've got plenty of time.'

I snuggle into Mum, breathing in her warm, sleepy smell and the sweet scent of her shampoo. For a moment it's like I'm six years old again.

'It's OK, Mum. I do want to do it.'

'Honest?' Mum says, smoothing my hair.

I pull away and flash her a super-confident smile. 'I want to sing my songs, Mum. That's more important to me than anything else. I wouldn't miss out on this for anything.'

And it's true, I think, as I climb the stairs to go back to bed. Nothing is going to stop me from being brilliant tomorrow. And if that means wiping Twig from my memory, then that's what I'll do. I picture him one last time, his flop of hair hanging over his eyes, his funny smile, his soft voice. Then I press an imaginary DELETE button in my brain. That's it. He doesn't exist any more. He can't upset me any more. I'm not going to think about him any more.

I lie flat on my back in my bed and stare at the blackness. I have to do my best tomorrow. Better than my best. I need to knock their socks off at the recording studio. And I can't let a boy – any boy – get in the way of that, can I?

9

Well, this is it! Friday at last. Whoop! Whoop!

Miss Peabody looked distinctly green around the gills at Registration, then rushed out, her hand clamped over her mouth, making glubbing sounds like a haddock in a fishbowl. Rumour is that Mr Hemphead has moved in with her and is officially now her house-husband! So I suppose his cooking must be responsible.

Then in maths we had to write a definition of the properties of a triangle. And here's what I wrote:

What I know about triangles by Sassy Wilde
A triangle has three sides and three angles. These are called Cordelia, Taslima and Sassy. Triangles pop up all the time in the construction of bridges and buildings and things. This is because the triangle is a strong shape. It does not break easily. Which is what makes it the perfect shape for a friendship.

At three o'clock Taslima and Cordelia offer to walk with me to the main entrance where the Y-Gen car is coming to collect me. I pick up my rucksack and sling my guitar over my shoulder.

'Remember to do that visualization exercise before you perform,' Taslima advises as we walk round to the front of the school. 'Think successful and you'll be successful.' Taslima intends writing self-motivation books as well as being a psychologist.

'Yeah.' Cordelia narrows her green eyes at me. 'We're counting on you, Sass. Come back with a recording contract or we'll never speak to you again.'

'There's no pressure, then?' I smile weakly.

'Course not.' Cordelia flashes a wicked grin. 'Just be yourself. You'll blow them away.'

'And we'll send you positive vibes later,' Taslima reassures me. The thing is, I'm missing out on our usual Friday night sleepover at her house this week. Ben figures we won't be finished till nine at the earliest, so we wouldn't get back till ten. And cos Taslima's mum's really strict there's no way I can turn up on her doorstep that late. But I'm happy enough. I can't have everything, can I? And I know that me and Cordelia and Taslima will have zillions of other sleepovers.

As we wander to the front of the building, I glance across to the wall where A CERTAIN BOY used to sit and wait for me. (OK, so the DELETE button in my brain didn't work, but it was worth a try.)

It's daft, I know, but I really, really hoped he would be there today. That he would've realized how stupid it is to fall out over a silly misunderstanding and that he would've turned up to wish me luck.

I try to pretend I'm not looking for him. But Cordelia looks at Taslima, and Taslima looks at me, and what with one being psychic, and the other a psychologist, I guess they both know what I'm thinking.

As we wait at the main car park Megan appears. When she links arms with me I try not to pull back. Megan, Taslima figures, is lonely and confused since her parents divorced and Twig and his dad moved in. Taslima says we should let her hang out with us till she gets her self-confidence back. I can see what Tas is getting at, but to be honest I liked it better when it was just Cordelia, her and me. You know, the perfect friendship triangle.

Just then something whizzes past our heads and lands at Cordelia's feet. Followed closely by Midge Murphy.

'Sorry, ladies,' Midge grins as he retrieves his shoe. His mates are standing a short distance away, hooting with laughter.

'Attention-seeking behaviour,' Taslima sighs. 'A sign of immaturity in the male of the species.'

Then Magnus materializes at my side. 'So, Sassy, when will you be back?'

Before I can answer, a huge black Hummer with dark-tinted glass windows swings into the school car park and pulls up just behind Miss Cassidy's little Ka.

'Oh no!' I groan. 'They said they'd send a CAR!'

'Is *that* for you?' Magnus asks, wide-eyed.

'I hope not,' I mutter, as the driver's door opens and Ben leaps down and stretches like he's been driving for hours.

'Hi, Sassy!' he waves cheerily. 'Gorgeous day, isn't it?'

Before I can reply, Magnus grabs my guitar and ruckie and heads across to the Hummer.

'I thought you were sending a CAR for me,' I say pointedly to Ben as I follow Magnus across.

'Turned out I had to go over to Glasgow earlier,' he explains. 'I was coming past this way anyway . . . so I called the office, got them to cancel the car, decided to pick you up personally.'

'This is the latest model, isn't it?' Magnus interrupts, his face glowing. It is SO sad. He's obviously impressed by the big shiny thing on wheels. Megan rolls her eyes. Taslima takes out her notebook and makes a quick note. I know she's been doing a psychological profile on Magnus. It's clear he thinks Ben's big shiny machine is the best thing ever.

'Yep,' says Ben, banging his hand against the bonnet like it was a horse. 'Best on the market. Six-speed automatic transmission. Two overdrive gears. Six-point-two-litre engine. You can take this little baby anywhere.'

'Little baby!' I gasp. 'That . . . that . . . THING . . . is hardly a little baby. It's a huge ugly polluting gas-guzzling –' I stop mid-sentence. They're not even listening to me! Ben has opened the door. Magnus has dropped my guitar and rucksack and has his head stuck inside, gazing at the instrument panel.

Just then Miss Cassidy arrives, laden down with bags and followed by two senior boys carrying big boxes.

'I don't know how so much of my own stuff ends up in school every week,' she groans as she opens the boot and folds the seats of the little Ka down. 'OK, boys,' she says. 'Just bung all that stuff in.'

She takes a deep breath, straightens her skirt and looks at me, then at the Big Shiny Black Thing on Wheels, then at Ben, who's still showing his 'little baby' off to Magnus.

'And you are?' Miss Cassidy says, scowling.

'Ben,' Ben grins. 'Y-Gen Music.' He pulls a card from his shirt pocket and passes it to Miss Cassidy. 'I'm here to pick up young Sassy.'

'And I really don't want to take a lift in THAT!'

I sigh. 'Everyone knows how I feel about huge four-wheel drives. They go completely against my eco-principles.'

Magnus, who's been walking round the Big Black Shiny Thing on Wheels like he's in a car showroom, reappears just then.

'Will I put Sassy's stuff in the back for you?' he asks eagerly.

'No!' I growl. 'You will not!' It's pitiful! It is so obvious he wants an excuse to open the boot.

'Look, Sassy,' Ben says, a sharp edge in his voice. 'Do you want to go to the recording studio or not? Because really I don't have time –'

'Excuse me!' Miss Cassidy interrupts. 'I think Sassy has a point. I mean, you don't need to drive a huge thing like that . . . unless, of course, you do tons of off-road . . .' She looks him slowly up and down. His flash sunglasses, his loose silk shirt, his expensive designer jeans. 'You're not a farmer, are you?'

There's a small crowd gathered round now. Cordelia, Megan and Taslima are still waiting to see me off. Like iron filings to a magnet, Midge, Beano and Karim Malik have been attracted by the Big Shiny Black Thing on Wheels. The two seniors who helped load up Miss Cassidy's Ka are all ears.

'No, I'm not a farmer,' Ben says coldly. 'But I *am* busy. And I need to get going, so –'

'Maybe I could take Sassy,' Miss Cassidy says brightly. 'Where's she going?'

'Edinburgh,' Ben says.

Miss Cassidy's brow furrows. 'Well, it's quite a bit off my way, but I suppose I could –'

'Pffff!' Magnus interrupts. 'How does that make sense? I mean, Ben's going where Sassy's going anyway. If you go there, Miss, and it's not where you were actually going, then that makes more carbon emissions than if Sassy just took the lift from Ben in the first place . . . doesn't it?'

Magnus looks at me as if he's expecting me to give him a gold star for saying something environmentally friendly. Taslima nods wisely and makes a quick note in her notebook.

'And in any case, Miss Cassidy,' says one of the seniors, eyeing my guitar in its humungous airport case, 'you'll never fit THAT *and* Sassy into your little Ka.'

Miss Cassidy looks at the junk piled high in the back of her tiny car.

'I suppose Magnus has a point, Sassy,' she says. 'As Ben's here already, it probably makes sense to take the lift THIS time. No one's going to think any worse of you for taking the occasional lift in a Hummer. Sometimes you have to compromise.'

So that's what I do. Compromise. Taslima, Cordelia and Megan give me one last good luck hug, then, with a heavy heart, I climb up into the front seat beside Ben. I'm just about to pull the door shut when Magnus pops his head in.

'Actually,' Magnus says to Ben, 'you have to pass my house to get to the motorway. You couldn't give me a lift, could you?'

'Sure, kid,' Ben nods. 'Glad somebody's happy to ride with me. Hop in beside Sassy!'

As he climbs up into the front seat I'm forced to slide into the middle. Magnus grins as he helps me find the central seat belt and fasten it. 'See, I'm getting the hang of this environmentally friendly thing,' he grins. 'We can all share our carbon emissions. Save the planet.'

I fire him a filthy look, but already he's playing with the window controls. The tinted glass slides down. Then Ben starts the engine and we're off. Taslima, Cordelia, Megan and Miss Cassidy all stand waving goodbye.

As we swing out of the car park I'm thinking that maybe I need to be less hard on myself, maybe I do need to soften up a bit, maybe I take the whole environmental-consciousness-green thing too seriously.

And that's when I see A CERTAIN BOY, sitting on the wall, watching, as I'm driven away with Magnus, in the biggest, ugliest, greediest Big Shiny Thing on Wheels imaginable.

10

Why did Twig have to be there today just when I'd given in and got into Ben's Hummer? Now he'll think I've sold out completely, that I just happily climbed in and drove off. And he'll think that he was right, that I've given up everything I believe in just so I can get my chance at fame.

Ben and Magnus chat away while I sit jammed between them in a big unhappy sulk. Magnus, apparently, has just become interested in the music business. 'I wouldn't mind doing music management when I'm older,' he tells Ben, and I try not to snort with derision. I know for a fact Magnus isn't into music at all. He even gets off music every week to do weightlifting sessions as part of his swim-training.

At the edge of town when we stop at the end of Magnus's street, Ben flicks a business card from his shirt pocket. 'If you decide to get into the music business, Magnus, give me a call,' Ben says. 'We can always use the right kind of person.'

As he gets out Magnus turns and gives me a thumbs up, 'Good luck, Sassy,' he says. 'You'll blow them away. I know you will.'

'Cool guy,' Ben says as Magnus saunters off and we pull out into the traffic.

'Whatever,' I mutter.

'You OK, kiddo?' Ben glances across at me. 'Not nervous, are you?'

I take a deep breath. I'm not OK. I would be OK if Twig was talking to me, if Twig had given me a thumbs up and had wished me luck. But he didn't, did he?

'Nervous? No way! Just a bit sleepy, that's all.' I force a yawn and stretch for added effect.

'Relax, then,' Ben says, turning the radio on. 'You've got a busy time ahead of you.'

From the outside the recording studio looks like a big old Victorian house, set back from the road in its own grounds in a leafy suburb of Edinburgh.

Zing makes a huge fuss when I arrive, like I'm a star already, which does make me feel better about things. There are framed photos in the hallway too of all the Y-Gen success stories, including Phoenix Macleod.

'Phoenix was our last signing on the Y-Gen label,' Zing explains as she shows me into a changing room with a huge lit-up mirror and its own toilet and shower. 'We're very selective, you know. We're only interested in the best!'

My heart starts to race when Zing says that. Because that's what I want to be. The best. And I'm going to sing my heart out to prove it.

Zing flashes me a super-white smile as she leaves. 'Freshen up, then come through to the kitchen when you're ready,' she says. Then she's gone. I look around. Is it possible Phoenix Macleod once used this changing room? A shiver of excitement shimmies right through me.

Quickly, I change out of my school polo shirt and skirt and pull on a vest-top and a pair of jeans. As soon as I get out of that silly uniform I start to feel much more confident, more like myself, much more grown-up. I'm just fixing my hair in the mirror and putting on a teensy bit of make-up – a bit of gloss on my lips and a bit of mascara – when my eye catches my friendship bracelet. I finger it thoughtfully for a moment. I suppose I should take it off. I mean, if Twig's not friends with me any more, I shouldn't really be wearing his bracelet, should I? A big feeling of sadness wells up inside me as I pick at the knot. But it's no use. Since Twig tied it on I've been wearing it non-stop – even in the bath and in the shower – and all the little threads have become moulded into one. There's no way the knot can be picked apart.

'Are you ready yet?' Zing pops her smiley face round the door. I really like Zing. She's so upbeat. If you shook her, I bet she'd fizz up like a bottle of champagne and explode with laughter.

In the kitchen I meet Andy, the sound recorder. He's a big fierce-looking guy with long straggly hair and tattoos. Exactly what I think a roadie for some sort of heavy-metal band would look like. Scary! But when he speaks his voice is gentle.

Zing offers me a choice of kiddie snacks and a six-pack of Mister Men juice she's bought in especially. Honestly! She must think I'm about six! I take a carton of juice,[8] but I'm way too nervous to eat anything.

Then, at last, we're in the recording studio!

I can't believe it. I have dreamed about this moment so often. Andy sits behind a big glass window in front of these huge soundboards with hundreds of dials and flashing lights, completely cut off from the main part of the studio.

'Don't worry about any of this stuff,' Andy says as he shows me the soundboards. 'This lot's for me to take care of.'

Then Ben leads me through to the recording space. There are no windows anywhere and it's completely soundproofed so when we record there'll be no unwanted noises, like birds or traffic

---

[8] Mr Bump, if you must know.

or the wind. I notice several beautiful guitars on stands. A big drum kit. Even a baby grand piano.

'Do you play?' Zing asks when I run my fingers over the piano keys.

'Only this,' I say, and quickly pick out a plonky version of 'Twinkle, Twinkle Little Star'.

Everyone laughs and I relax a bit. 'Maybe you should stick to the guitar!' Ben smiles.

I pick my guitar up and walk over to where there's a mike on a stand with a round mesh screen thing in front of it.

'Are you OK?' Zing asks, adjusting the mike so it's at the right height for me. My stomach clenches.

'Sure,' I grin.

'We're not recording right away,' Ben reassures me. 'We just want you to get the feel of the place. Relax into it. Just sing us through a few of your songs.'

Nervously, I start to tune up. This all feels so weird. Ben and Zing go behind the glass with Andy, then Ben's voice comes through the intercom.

'Think of this as a bit of fun, Sassy,' he advises. 'Imagine you're alone in your room. Try to forget we're here.'

I finish tuning and look up. The studio's totally quiet, eerily so. Like you could reach out a hand and actually grab a fistful of silence. Through the glass, Andy's head is down, his brow furrowed as he concentrates on his soundboards. I can see Ben and Zing chatting away to each other, though I can't hear a thing.

I take a deep, calming breath, close my eyes and do the visualization exercise Taslima taught me. I see me. On stage in front of a huge crowd. I'm singing and they're loving it. I reach the end of my song and I can hear the roar of the crowd in my ears. Then I snap my eyes open. All the negativity I felt in the Hummer is gone. I'm going to give this recording 100 per cent!

My hands stop shaking and my tummy settles. I play a couple of chords. I don't want to start with something they've not heard before, so I decide on 'When the Little Birds Stopped Singing'. You know, the song they first heard on the Internet clip, the one that was secretly filmed.[9]

After the first few lines I lose myself in the melody. In my head I'm back up the tree again with Twig . . . I'm in my room singing it for Twig . . . I'm thinking about Twig.

And then it's over.

The silence descends once more. Wrapping around me like a thick invisible blanket.

'That sounded great, kiddo.' Ben's voice comes through the intercom. 'Andy's got the sound levels

[9] I wish I knew who did it. I must ask Cordelia if she's got any hunches.

now. Just play what you want. Relax into it. Have fun!'

And that's how the next hour goes. Ben keeps saying, 'That's great, kiddo. Do us another.'

About seven o'clock we take a break. Ben and Zing both say they're delighted with how I'm coming across in the studio. I phone Mum and let her know I'm fine. Mum's just home from Pip's play and I can hear Pip stressing in the background. 'She's lost one of her false eyelashes,' Mum confides. 'I'd better go and calm her down.'

False eyelashes! Pip already has the most gorgeous dark curly eyelashes. I have tried so hard to instil some sense into that child. I dread to think what she's going to be like by the time she's a teen.

After the break – and a Mr Tickle juice – we go back into the recording studio. Ben says they're ready to cut a short demo, then we can finish up. He's asked me to choose three songs that show the range of what I can do.

'How about "When the Little Birds Stopped Singing", "I Don't Want To Be a Juliet to Your Romeo" and "Sweatshop Kid"?' I suggest.

'OK, we'll go with that,' Ben grins.

The first two songs go great. Zing's all smiles and Ben looks serious but impressed.

Then I start a run-through of 'Sweatshop Kid',

and I'm mid-way through the third verse when Zing's voice breaks in over the intercom.

'Thanks, Sassy. I don't think we'll use that one. Have you something else you can let us hear?'

'But I was wanting this one on my demo. I think it's one of my best. It's got a great chorus. Really catchy.'

'It needs a bit more work, Sassy,' Zing insists in a sharp no-more-nonsense voice that doesn't suit her at all. 'Personally, I don't think it's one of your best. Not right for a demo at any rate.'

I sigh noisily and roll my eyes.

'If you're going to make it in this business, you need to be able to accept advice, Sassy,' Ben says quietly. '*Without* rolling your eyes.'

I roll my eyes again. And smile cheekily. They both laugh.

'OK,' I say. 'But I still think "Sweatshop Kid" is a really good song.'

'No one's saying it's not,' Ben reasons. 'But we're trying to put together a demo here. It's a showcase. Trust our professional judgement. We've been doing this a long time. OK?'

'I suppose so,' I say and pick up my guitar again. 'So what do you want me to sing?'

'Some kind of love song, maybe?' Zing says over the intercom. 'Something about being young, heartbroken, suicidal . . . That sort of thing.'

I think for a minute. I do have a kind of love

song. It's been forming in my head ever since the blow-out with Twig, and it fits to a chord sequence I've practised quite a lot. I strum my guitar a few times. Just thinking about Twig is painful, so if it's broken-hearted they want, then that's what they're going to get.

We like the same things,
we share the same laughs
You think that I'm kooky,
I think that you're daft
I love when you're waiting
out by the school gate
And when you're not there,
my heart starts to break.

If only you'd call
It might all be all right
What can I say
To make things OK
You thought I was wrong
I thought I was right
You were sweet
You were cool
And I was a fool . . .

I glance up at the glass. Ben's looking thoughtful. Zing's smiling in a sad, dreamy way.

I wish that you'd call me,
I wish that you'd phone

And that's when the most amazing thing happens. My mobile rings! I stop mid-phrase.

The ringing in my pocket grows louder. On the other side of the glass Zing throws her arms up in exasperation. Ben leans forward to the mike and his voice, calm but cool, comes over the intercom.

'You may as well answer it now, Sassy.'

I stick my guitar on the stand and fumble in my pocket.

I glance at the number. It's not Cordelia. It's not Taslima. It's not Mum. It's not Dad. But it is a Strathcarron number. My heart starts to beat fast. Maybe, just maybe, it's Twig? Maybe somehow, in some kind of psychic way, he's connected with my song and now he's calling to say he's sorry, and I'll say, no, it was me that was in the wrong . . .

I press the answer button.

'Hi, Sassy!' The line buzzes like a wasp's caught in it.

'Twig?' I say, my heart in my mouth.

'Twig?' The voice crackles, then suddenly the line clears. 'Course not! It's Magnus. Listen, Sassy, I was thinking, there's a great film on at the cinema tomorrow, and I wondered –'

I stab an angry finger at the 'end call' button. Then turn the mobile off and stuff it back in my pocket. Tears prick my eyes. Tears of anger that Magnus has the cheek to call me and ask me out. Tears of frustration that it wasn't Twig.

'Ready for another take?' Ben's voice booms in the silent space.

I nod towards the glass booth, close my eyes for a second to centre myself in the song, then start up again.

I start it gently like last time. Then, without meaning to, I start to sing louder, start to play faster. My frustration, my disappointment, my hurt flood down my arm and into the chords. Hurt fills my voice. Tears trickle down my face.

When I finish I drop my head in emotional exhaustion.

At last I look up. Andy's grinning through the glass. 'Brilliant, Sass! We've got that in one. Great stuff!'

He gives me a thumbs up, then goes back to fiddling with his soundboards. Zing opens the door into the recording space and comes bouncing across, beaming, and offers me a handful of tissues. 'Way to go, Sass!' she enthuses. 'Maybe we should let you keep your mobile on every time you record!'

'It wasn't bad news, was it?' Ben asks, concerned.

I shake my head and force a laugh. 'No, not really.'

'Well, you were awesome, kiddo.' Ben ruffles my hair. 'Whoever called you, you certainly owe them one! Why don't you call back and say thanks?'

'It's OK.' I shove my guitar back into its travel case and clip it shut. 'It was just a nuisance call.'

11

We finish much earlier than Ben expected.

'With some people recording can take so much longer,' Zing says as she places my guitar in the boot of her car. Zing has agreed to drive me home so I don't need to get into Ben's big Hummer ever again. 'You were great in the studio. Well done!'

'So does that mean you'll offer me a recording deal?' I ask cheekily as I strap myself into the front seat.

Zing laughs. 'Oh, it's not just us who decide,' she explains as we drive off. 'There's a whole crowd of people who make that decision. We'll let them hear your demo, then we'll get back to you.'

While Zing drives I use the last of my credit to phone home to ask if it's OK if Zing drops me off at Taslima's. Zing says we should be back in Strathcarron before nine and I figure that's not too late – even for Taslima's mum! I've also decided not to think any more about Twig. He's the PAST. My music is my future, and I'm so excited about getting the demo done I want to share everything with my two best buds right away. I really can't wait till morning to see them.

Dad's great. If Zing takes me straight to Taslima's, he says he'll bring my overnight stuff round just after nine.

It's only ten to nine as I wave goodbye to Zing and hurry up the path to Taslima's house.

'Surprise!' I grin as Taslima opens the door. 'I didn't have any more credit, or I'd have called first!'

Taslima's face clouds. And I'm just wondering why, when who should appear at her shoulder but Megan! All my excitement fizzles away as Megan beams at me and says, 'Hi, Sassy! How did it go?'

'OK,' I mutter as I follow Taslima through to the living room to say hello to her mum. I don't know what to think. Do Taslima and Cordelia feel they have to replace me if I'm not there for five minutes? Or does Megan just have the knack of wriggling her way into my space as soon as my back's turned?

'Ah, Sassy!' Mrs Ankhar says. 'This is a surprise. I thought you were not coming this evening.' Then she looks sternly at Taslima. 'You are remembering the sleepover rule?'

Taslima's face burns as she nods her head. Mrs

Ankhar has a rule – well, actually, Mrs Ankhar has a gazillion rules – and the sleepover rule is that Taslima can have no more than two friends at a time.

'Don't worry, Mrs Ankhar,' I say quickly, even as my heart bombs into my boots. 'I'm going home soon. My dad's coming for me.'

As Taslima leads me upstairs, I wish I had never decided to come round her house. It was a stupid idea. I realize that now.

Silently we file into Taslima's room. Three plates sit on a tablecloth on the floor, piled high with Mrs Ankhar's deliciously mouth-watering pakora and bhajis. Three of Mrs Ankhar's hand-embroidered napkins lie crumpled beside them. Three bright tumblers of juice sit on Taslima's bedside table.

Megan bounces across the bed to make a space for me. I get this strange sensation, like they were all having a great time before I arrived.

'I'll run downstairs and get another plate,' Taslima says brightly, but I'm pretty sure she's embarrassed.

'Come on, Sassy!' says Cordelia, her face shining. 'Spill, girl! How did it go?'

'OK,' I stammer, trying to suppress the feelings of betrayal. 'Zing says they'll listen to the demo, then get in touch if they want to take things further.'

'That's awesome!' Megan gasps. 'I'm so happy for you!'

And I honestly don't think she realizes she doesn't belong here, in my friend's room, with my friends.

'But I'm getting these vibes,' Cordelia frowns and spreads her fingers wide. 'You're not 100 per cent happy, are you?'

'Course I am,' I laugh, but it comes out wrong. An ugly, brittle sound, like glass splintering. Tears sting the back of my eyes and I hate myself for being so easily hurt. 'Why wouldn't I be happy?' I say. 'I've just made my first demo. There's a chance Y-Gen might even sign me –'

'It's Twig, isn't it?' Cordelia interrupts, as Taslima comes back into the room and hands me a plate and napkin. 'Megan was just saying you need to sort things out with him.'

'I don't see why I should!' I splutter. 'He was in the wrong too –'

'But maybe he was in the wrong for the right reasons?' Megan blurts. 'I mean, he took a big risk taking his dad's camcorder, and then you just clean forgot all about him.'

'So it's not surprising he's a bit upset with you,' Cordelia sighs.

Then Cordelia and Megan and Taslima start arguing about me and Twig and what I should do. And suddenly it feels like *I'm* the one who doesn't belong. Like they're in a friendship bubble and I'm on the outside, bouncing off an invisible barrier.

For a split second it flies through my brain that this is all because I have this silly fixation with being a star. With recording my songs and getting famous. That my life would be much better if the Y-Gen people had never called round last week. That I should have settled for being ordinary old Sassy Wilde, then Megan wouldn't be here. I'd still be friends with Twig. None of this would be happening.

'Listen, Sassy,' Taslima says. 'We think you should talk to Twig –'

'Look, can we change the subject?' I mutter. 'Twig's made it clear he doesn't want to see me –'

'That's SO not true,' Megan protests. 'He went round to school especially to see you this after-noon. And, omigod, he was *so* upset when he saw you and Magnus in that Hummer. Before I came out he was banging about the house, saying he hated it in Strathcarron and he was going back to live with his mum –'

'Please stop it, Megan!' I blurt. 'You're just making everything worse . . . and . . .' I try not to say them but the words slip past me like darting fish and no way can I stop them. 'And you shouldn't even be here!'

Megan's face crumples and tears spring up in her eyes. She jumps up from the bed and dashes for the door.

The bedside table rocks and the three glasses topple. Juice spills everywhere. Taslima and Cordelia grab napkins and start mopping furiously. I clench my eyes tight shut. Taslima's mum is so uptight about her room being 'nice', about us being 'nice'. Now she'll be in big trouble and it will be all my fault and she'll hate me forever.

'Is everything all right up there, girls?' Mrs Ankhar calls from the foot of the stairs. Taslima takes a deep breath and goes out on to the landing. Megan's locked in the toilet and there are little snuffly sounds coming from behind the door.

'Megan choked on a bit of bhaji, that's all,' Taslima calls down. 'She'll be OK in a minute.'

Then she comes back into the room and stares at me. 'You should have let Megan finish,' she says quietly. 'She stuck up for you with Twig. She told him what a fuss you made when Ben came for you in the Hummer.'

'Then she asked him if he wanted to make up with you,' says Cordelia. 'And he said yes.'

'But maybe you need to make up with Megan first?' Taslima sits on the bed beside me and puts an arm round my shoulder. 'Sassy, you're our friend. But Megan's lonely. That's why I asked her over tonight. She's doing her best to fit in, to make you like her. Give her a break, please?'

And I'm thinking that it's all very well for Taslima to feel like that, but *I'm* the one Megan hurt. OK, so I know she apologized a while back, but –

Just then Megan comes back into the room. She sits down carefully on the edge of the bed, biting her lip to keep the tears back. Taslima gives me a meaningful look and I know what she wants me to do.

'Sorry, Megan,' I say quietly.

'No worries!' Megan smiles shakily, 'you're a friend, aren't you?' She leans over and wraps me in a big hug.

And I can't help it, but there's no way I can make myself really hug her back.

I swear I have never felt so bad in my whole entire life.

12

The next morning I don't wake till almost eleven.

'I thought I was doing you a favour!' Mum objects when I grumble as I make a zingy wake-me-up smoothie. 'You were more tired than you know last night. I don't think you've been sleeping properly all week. It's just as well you came home.'

I yawn and press the button on the smoothie-maker. It roars into life, drowning out anything else Mum's saying. I hate to admit it, but she's right, I was pretty exhausted. Even so I didn't go straight to sleep. I thought about the Megan thing for a while and decided to do my best to be nice to her. See what happens. Then I thought about Twig. And I made a decision. I'm going to get this smoothie in me, then pretty myself up and go round to see him. Sort things out. I mean, there are enough wars in the world already without me and Twig joining in.

Pip's sitting at the kitchen table, brooding over a bowl of yogurt and strawberries. I plonk myself down beside her. 'What's wrong with you?' I ask, yawning.

Pip pokes at the strawberries with her spoon. 'Mum's insisting on force-feeding me! Like one of those Suffer-Jets!'

'What?' I ask.

'Suffer-Jets. You know, those women who fought so we could get equal rights and things and not be bossed around!'

'Suffragettes,' I correct her, slurping my smoothie. 'And I think Mum's right, Pip. You should eat breakfast every day. The Suffragettes fought for you to get the right to vote, not the right to starve yourself. And strawberries and yogurt aren't going to make you fat. It's chips and choccies that are evil.'

'Mmmph!' Pip says, licking delicately at a strawberry.

Just then Dad comes bouncing into the kitchen. Mum lowers her latest self-help book, *Your Inner Goddess, and How to Find Her*, and peers at him over her glasses.

'OK, girls,' he beams. 'Pretty yourselves up. We're going to Great-Gran's.'

What!!

'Can't we leave Great-Gran's till next weekend?' I ask, alarmed. Dad's already filling Brewster's dog bowl with fresh water and fetching a few chews to keep him busy while we're gone.

'Sorry, Sass,' Dad says cheerily. 'Great-Gran might be dead –'

'ANGUS!' Mum chucks a tea towel at him.

He ducks and it lands on Brewster. 'We've been putting this off for weeks, Sassy. Your mother and I decided last night. We're going today. All of us. No exceptions. No excuses.'

Pip and I exchange a glance. Instant allies once again. Honestly! My father might be a politician, but sometimes he forgets that young people have rights too!

'Shouldn't we be part of the decision-making process?' I protest. 'I mean, this is a democracy, isn't it?'

Pip nods her head vigorously. Encouraged, I continue to make our case. 'As daughters of reduced age, we may not have the vote.[10] But our rights are protected under the United Nations Convention on the Rights of the Child. And you haven't even asked me and Pip if we have other plans for today!'

'OK.' Mum cuts in. 'Pip! Sassy! Do you have other plans for today?'

Ooops. I wasn't expecting that. I've been so carried away with formulating the next bit of my speech – about how parents should have to go up for election every year and then we could vote them out if we felt they weren't treating us fairly

[10] Yet!

– I haven't worked out a suitable fib to tell them. The last thing I'm going to say is that I want to go round and make up with Twig.

'Study?' I say hopefully.

'Sassy, since when have you ever wanted to study when you don't have to?' Mum laughs. 'So I call this debate to a close. We're all going to Great-Gran's. Go get showered. Now!'

Half an hour later we're all in the car. Pip is in an almighty huff. Mum has insisted on making her dress like a nine-year-old. Which I have to say, I think she should be doing anyway.

'Great-Gran's heart's not very strong,' Mum insisted as she tugged one of my old cotton frocks over Pip's head. 'She thinks you're a sweet little girl, and I want her to continue thinking that. So no make-up either!'

'Can't I put on a teensy bit of lipgloss?' Pip pouted as Mum dragged her out to the car.

'When will we be back?' I ask as I strap myself in.

'Stop moaning!' Dad says, which I think is pretty unfair. All I did was ask a reasonable question! 'We should be back by about seven. You can have the whole evening to yourself.'

Great-Gran lives over a hundred miles away. Which, in one way, is a blessing as she's not the easiest Great-Gran to get on with. But it does mean a long boring car journey.

Pip and I snuggle down in the back. We're well prepared. I slouch low in the seat, pop my earplugs in, switch on my fave sounds. Pip gets out a sketchbook and her coloured marker pens. (Her teacher told her recently she's good at art, so she's decided she's going to be a fashion designer.) Mum yawns. Dad puts his sunglasses on, starts the engine, and we're off.

And I'm off too.

To sleep.

ZZZZZZZZZZZZZZZZZZZZZZZZZZZZZ
ZZZZZZZZZZZZZZZZZZZZZZZZZZZZZZ
ZZZZZZZZZZZZZZZZZZZZZZZZZZZZZZZZZZ
ZZZZZZZZZZZZZZZZZZZZZZZZZZZZZZZZZZZZZZZ
ZZZZZZZZZZZZZZZZ

Suddenly I'm lurched rudely awake as the car swerves. Dad slams on the brakes and we judder to a halt. Blinking against the sudden daylight, I tug out my earplugs – just as a police car slews across in front of us, blue lights flashing. It emits one long final wail and a policeman leaps out, rushes over, pulls Dad's door open and shouts: **'OUT OF THE CAR! NOW!'**

Dad stumbles out, looking totally confused. So am I. Dad *never* speeds. We're lucky if we ever get over forty. The officer hollers at Dad to lean over the bonnet of the car, his hands clasped behind his back. Wow! I've heard stories about police being heavy-handed, but this all seems a bit extreme!

There's a police officer at Mum's door too. A woman. She orders Mum out in a fierce voice and sends her to sit in the back of the police car. The passing traffic slows as people try to see what's going on. The policeman's frisking Dad like he thinks he might be armed.

Then the policewoman opens Pip's door. 'Don't be scared,' she says, suddenly all soft and smiley. 'You're safe now. Everything's going to be all right.'

Pip's face is deathly white. 'I think there's . . . maybe . . . been a . . . misunderstanding . . .' Pip stammers in a tiny voice.

'It's all right, poppet,' the policewoman says kindly. 'You don't need to lie. They can't hurt you now.'

I pinch myself, sure that I'm trapped in some weird kind of dream where I think I'm awake but I'm not. But nothing changes.

Then Pip turns round and, her hand shaking, removes a sheet of drawing paper from the back window.

The policewoman takes it from her, and as she does, I realize why Pip is suddenly so pale. In her childish scrawl, in bright red letters, it says:

HELP! CALL POLICE. IM BEING KIDNAPED!

13

I could kill Pip!

So could Mum. And Dad. We all have to go to the police station to clear up the 'misunderstanding'. When Dad insists, little puffs of steam coming from his ears, that he's a Very Important Person – an MP no less – and questions will be raised in Parliament about the ridiculous way he's been treated, the police officer says, 'Child abduction is a very serious issue, sir. If we didn't act on 999 calls from the public you would raise questions in Parliament about that too, I suppose?'

Dad shuts up after that.

Mum is so angry she can't speak. Her hair has frizzled up with rage and her face is an alarming magenta colour.

Pip is blubbering.

I am fuming. I got up this morning with one simple plan. One thing I wanted to do. Go round to see Twig and sort things out. But instead, thanks to my despotic parentals and my dysfunctional little sis, here I am, stuck in a police station like a common criminal.

At last they let us go.

We climb into the car in a silence so tense you could trampoline on it. Mum takes Pip's sketchbook and coloured pens. 'I think I'll have these,' she says. 'Before you get any other daft ideas.'

Dad starts the engine.

'Good!' I say. 'Can we go home now?'

'We set out this morning to go to Great-Gran's,' Dad growls. 'And that's what we're doing.'

'But I'm traumatized!' I complain.

'We're all traumatized,' Mum says. 'It's not Great-Gran's fault she's got a delinquent for a great-grandchild.' She fires an angry look at Pip. But Pip is already recovering. She pops her earphones in and gazes serenely out of the window.

I sit back and go over in my head once again just what I'm going to say to Twig when I at last get the chance to see him.

The visit to Great-Gran's lasts, I think, roughly a thousand years. It's a gorgeous summer's day, but Great-Gran's like a bat. Or a vampire.[11] She doesn't like the sun. She says we'll all get skin

---

[11] Without the teeth.

cancer if we sit out. And then we'll be sorry. We'll not live to a ripe old age like her.[12]

So we are forced to sit in her gloomy living room – with the central heating on full blast, which is SO irresponsible and must be contributing MASSIVELY to global warming – drinking watery juice, listening to her wittering on and on and on and on about all her friends who've died recently.

Then she starts up about her gallstones. Don't ask me what gallstones are! But Great-Gran's are playing up.

Her toenails are a problem too. Turning against her, they are.

And then there's the paper boy. Keeps delivering the *Mail* when she wants the *Express*. 'What is it with young people nowadays?' Great-Gran says, fixing me with her fierce stare, like I am *personally* responsible. 'Don't they teach you to read any more?'

This is not one of Great-Gran's good days.

Don't get me wrong. I love my great-gran. But I find it really, really hard to sit in her living room on a brilliant sunny afternoon listening to all her moans and medical details when I absolutely

---

[12] I'm not sure I want to live till I'm THAT old. I mean, what is the point! Great-Gran is the best ad for dying young I could think of.

totally seriously need to go round to Twig's and get my love life back on track.

At last Great-Gran decides she's had enough of us. Which is just as well as I swear a thin layer of dust has settled over me and I have lost the will to live.

'Do you lot not have anything better to do with your time than clutter up my house?' she grumbles. Pip and I don't wait about. We hug her hugely like she's our most fave person on the planet, then dash for the door.

Free! Free! Free at last! So this is what Nelson Mandela felt like when he was released from Robyn Island after twenty-seven years of imprisonment. I turn my face up to the sun and feel its golden life-giving caress.

It's all I can do to stop from cheering as we climb back into the car and wave goodbye. Mum chides, 'Wait till you're Great-Gran's age, Sassy, and then you'll know what it's like!'

By the time we get home it's almost nine o'clock. I say I'm nipping round to see Megan and Twig, which is not quite a lie, is it? I promise I'll just be half an hour.

'OK,' Mum shouts as Dad pours her a glass of wine to calm her nerves. 'But make sure you are. We've had more than enough drama for one day!'

As I walk up the path to Twig's house, I peer up

into the tree where he was that first night I met him. I gaze deep into the thick green leaves, sort of hoping to see his face grinning back at me.

Then I take a deep breath, press the buzzer and wait.

Megan's mum opens the door.

'Sassy!' she exclaims. 'How lovely to see you! But Megan's out. Round at Taslima's. She's due back soon, if you want to come in.'

When she says 'round at Taslima's' this little jealousy-beast stirs inside me and bares its fangs, but I take it by the throat and squeeze and it retreats into a dark corner of my heart.

'Actually . . .' I force myself to smile. 'I was wondering if Twig's in?'

'Twig?' she echoes, and I feel my colour start to rise. Megan's mum's known me since I was in Nursery and whenever I speak to her I feel three years old again. Far too young to be asking after a boy. 'I'm sorry, Sassy. He's not. And I really don't know when he'll be back. In fact I've no idea where he even is. He's a law unto himself, that boy.'

'Oh!' I say, disappointed. 'Can you tell him I called?'

'Course I will!' Mrs Campbell smiles. 'Oh, and Sassy,' she says as I turn to go, 'I'm so pleased you and Megan are friends again. She's been so much happier this last couple of weeks.'

And she closes the door.

14

My heart's heavy as I make my way down the path. If only my stupid parentals had let me go and see Twig this morning, instead of dragging me off to Great-Gran's, we might have made up by now.

And I'm thinking that this is one of those days where I should just have stayed in bed, when something small and hard bounces off my head and rolls along the path in front of me. A nut!

Even before I see where it's come from, this little bubble of hope starts to swell inside me.

As another nut ricochets off my skull, I pull a paper hankie from my pocket and wave it like a white flag. 'I come in peace,' I shout up into the branches above me.

'That's what I was hoping,' Twig says, swinging down from the tree and landing lightly beside me. 'So we're not at war any more?'

'Were we at war?'

'Sort of . . .' Twig says, hanging his head sheepishly. 'But the point is, I'm sorry.'

'*You're* sorry?' I gasp. 'No, it's me that's sorry.'

'I know,' he says. 'You told me that before. In the kitchen. Remember? When you had a blob of scooshy cream on your nose. But I'd got myself into such a bad place I just wouldn't listen. I shouldn't have –'

'I shouldn't have abandoned you for the Y-Gen people –'

'Look,' Twig interrupts. 'We could go on like this forever. Can we just put it behind us? Forget all about it?'

'Forget all about what?' I ask, smiling.

'Dunno,' he grins. 'I've forgotten. Anyway, what are you doing now?'

I check my watch. 'I pretty much have to go home. The parentals are in a foul mood. Pip's been grounded for a year.'

'So can I walk you home?' Twig asks shyly, and my heart sings.

'Sure,' I grin. 'The long way round, or through the woods?'

'Through the woods,' Twig says. And then he takes my hand. And I fill up with this big surge of happiness. And, you know, if Twig wasn't holding my hand I think I'd float right off, up into the sky. And take him with me, of course!

Some things are just too good to ever let go of.

15

The following morning birdsong wakes me. I blink my eyes open and turn to see the time. It's only half-past five but already it's bright daylight outside. I snuggle under the duvet and try to sleep. I was having a beautiful tropical island dream and I want to go back there. But I can't, can I? Because it was just a dream. And dreams aren't real life.

I turn over and watch the early morning light creep across the ceiling. I was so happy in my dream. There was just me and Twig on this tropical island and I sang my songs for him every night and everything was perfect. Taslima says that when we dream we're really working out things that are bothering us in our waking lives. She says we should listen to what our dreams are telling us. Which makes me wonder, am I making a mistake wanting to be a star? Maybe it's enough just to sing for the people I love. Maybe that's what the dream was trying to tell me.

When the grandfather clock in the hall booms

out seven o'clock I know I can't stay in bed any longer. I'm just not sleepy enough. In any case, there's a new song forming in my head. I get up and swish my curtains wide open. Little white fluffy clouds tinged with pink drift across a perfect blue sky. I get my notebook and sit cross-legged on my rainbow rug, then start scribbling.

Boy, I dream of being with you
Where the sea is warm and the sky is blue
I want to walk along the sand
I want to have you hold my hand
And every night when the sun sinks low
And the ocean flames with its orange glow
I want to sit with you high in a tree
And watch the moon rise over the sea
Cos, boy, I dream of being with you
I hope you dream of being with me . . .

It takes me a while to get the lines the way I want them, but even as I'm trying to get the rhymes this little melody starts to form in my head. I hum it softly as I scribble, then I try putting the two together. It's not quite there yet, but it's sort of coming. I pick my guitar up and cradle it across my lap, then I start strumming and trying to find some basic chords to fit. At last it comes together. I shove a blank tape in my music system and push the record button. I know I'll need to work on it more, but I also know there's something there. Something special. I'm halfway through when the door opens and Mum stands grinning down at me.

'Don't laugh at my songs!' I explode, my colour rising. It's almost like my mum has trespassed into one of my dreams! 'And KNOCK before you come bursting into my room!'

Mum rolls her eyes. 'Didn't you hear the phone?' she asks.

I shake my head and glance at my bedside clock. It's almost ten! I can hardly believe it.

'Anyway, it was Zing,' Mum continues, 'and guess what?'

Zing! The minute Mum says her name my heart starts to race like a hyperactive hamster in an exercise wheel.

'I don't want to guess, Mum. Just tell me quick. Please?' I squeeze the words out, high-pitched.

'Well,' says Mum, sitting on the edge of my bed, 'you left your purple hair scrunchie at the recording studio, and they're going to put it in the post.'

'Oh,' I say, this huge lump of disappointment bulging in my throat.

'And,' Mum continues, 'they're very interested in signing you, but –'

'Sorry, Mum. Can you say that bit again?'

'They're interested in signing you –'

'Oh My Jimminy Crimpets Joogledy Boogledy!'

I exclaim, throwing my guitar on the bed and hugging Mum.

'Don't you want to know what the "BUT" is?' Mum laughs, ruffling my hair.

'Not really,' I grin.

'OK.' Mum turns and heads for the door.

'No! No! I do! Please!' I grab hold of her sleeve. Through my head a hundred different ideas are galloping –

BUT we don't want to pay you.

BUT we want you to shave your head.

BUT we need you to take guitar lessons, singing lessons, dancing lessons, French lessons . . .

Mum looks suddenly serious. 'I think you'd better sit down,' she says.

Oh no! My heart almost stops. What if they want me to compromise? Like I've promised myself I will never do?

'So what is it?' I croak, my throat dry with nerves.

'BUT . . . they want to see . . .' Mum gazes at me with big concerned eyes. I grab a cushion and hug it to my chest cos I need something to hang on to.

'. . . you play live first. In front of an audience.'

'Play live?' I repeat. 'How will I ever get the chance to play live . . . ? Maybe the school will let me do a lunchtime concert,' I gabble excitedly. 'It's almost end of term –'

Mum shushes me. 'Apparently there's a music festival next weekend. Called something weird, like the Wiccaman?'

'Yeah!' I gasp. 'Phoenix Macleod's playing at it. Megan's been rabbitting on about how she'd love to go –' I stop mid-sentence as it hits me. 'You don't mean . . .'

Mum grins. 'Oh yes, I do! They want you to do a few songs at it, see how you cope in front of a crowd.'

'What?' I gasp. 'They want me to play at the Wiccaman?'

Mum looks at a piece of paper in her hand. 'I made a few notes,' she says. 'Y-Gen have one of their singers performing. That boy you just mentioned. Phoenix Macleod. They want you to do a few songs before he comes on.'

I sink down on my bed, my legs wibbly-wobbly as a jelly baby's.

'Pinch me,' I say dreamily. 'I think I must be dreaming.'

Mum nips me hard. 'Ouch!' I squeal.

'We have to call them back and let them know if you want to do this festival thingy,' Mum says. 'As soon as possible. So what do you think?'

'Of course I want to do it!' I squeal, bouncing up and down on my bed like I used to when I was three and over-excited.

Just then Pip comes in. 'What's all the noise about!' she complains.

'I'm going to sing at the Wiccaman!' I scream. 'With Phoenix Macleod!'

'Oh, is that all,' Pip says and flounces back out. 'Cos Houdini's trying to sleep and you've only gone and woken him!'

16

As soon as I recover from the shock I phone Cordelia.

'Stay right where you are!' Cordelia says. 'I'll call Taslima. We'll come straight round. Then you can tell us everything! This is so-o-o-o-o exciting!'

Minutes later they arrive at the front door and we all jump about in a group hug, Brewster barking at our ankles.

'Girls! Girls! Girls!' Mum shouts from the living room. 'Calm down, will you! I'm trying to call Angus and I can hardly hear myself!'

So we tumble into the kitchen and I pour us fizzy lemonade in champagne glasses and we chink them together.

'I just KNEW something like this was going to happen!' Cordelia grins. We all look at her quizzically.

'I borrowed Mum's crystal ball when she was out,' Cordelia explains. 'I was trying to find out what was going to happen over the summer hols, but all I kept seeing was this big crowd of people and flashing lights, so I guessed you were going to be appearing somewhere, Sass.'

Taslima and me exchange a look. We never can figure if Cordelia is serious about all this psychic business, or just great at kidding us.

'You are so lucky!' Cordelia looks all dreamy. 'I bet the festival will be wickedly awesomely brill. I'd love to go to something like that!'

'Well, who knows, maybe you will!' says Mum, appearing in the doorway and twirling an imaginary wand like a fairy godmother. 'I've spoken to Sassy's dad. And I've checked out the Wiccaman festival on the Internet, and here's what we've agreed. Angus is so busy with all his constituency work that we're not getting a proper summer holiday this year, and since this Friday's an In Service training day so you'd be off school anyway, I'm going to book a yurt –'

'A YURT?' says Pip, who's just arrived and set Houdini in his salad bowl in the centre of the table. 'What's a YURT?' She pops a grape in and it bounces off Houdini's head.

'It's a kind of tent thing,' Mum explains. 'Like the nomads on the Russian steppes use.'

Pip curls up her nose. Houdini demolishes the grape. Pip might fret about her own weight, but she's certainly not worrying about his. He's turning into the fattest hamster I've ever seen.

'But the point is,' Mum continues, ignoring Pip, 'the yurts are big – they can sleep up to eight. So, Sassy, you can bring some friends along and we'll make a long weekend of it, Friday to Sunday. It sounds super. Right beside the sea. What do you think?'

'That sounds fantastic!' Cordelia whoops. 'And I'm sure Mum will be OK about it. She's been moaning on about needing some time to herself!'

'I'll have to check with my parents,' Taslima says. 'And if you speak to them, Mrs Wilde, I'm sure they'll agree. I'd love to come. Thank you.'

'That is so brilliant!' I beam and throw my arms round Mum's neck. 'You're the best mum ever!'

'There's just one thing,' Taslima adds quietly. 'How many did you say the yurt sleeps, Mrs Wilde?'

'Eight,' Mum replies. 'So even with me and Pip – and we'll take Brewster of course – and Sassy and you and Cordelia, there's tons of room.'

'In that case,' Taslima says, looking from Cordelia to me, 'don't you think there's someone else you should invite, Sassy?'

I drop my eyes. I know who she means.

'Taslima has a point,' Cordelia says. 'Megan's absolutely crazy about Phoenix Macleod. It would be mean to just go off without her. If there's space, that is.'

Mum looks at me. 'It's your call, Sass.'

And I tussle again with the fierce little jealousy-beast that raises its hackles whenever Megan's name's mentioned.

'Think about it, Sassy,' Taslima says in her soft voice. 'How would you feel if Megan, me and Cordelia went off without inviting you?'

I flinch when Taslima says that. I want to say, *but that's different, Taslima. You, me and Cordelia are best buds. I would have a right to be hurt if you went off with Megan without me.*

But in another way I know Taslima's right. It would be really mean not to at least *invite* Megan – though a bit of me still hopes she won't be able to come and things will be the way they were before, just me and my two best mates.

'OK,' I say at last, and the jealousy-beast sulks off, defeated, into the darkness. And then I have a brainwave! In fact, I don't know why I didn't think of it before. 'But if Megan comes can Twig come too?'

'No way!' Mum laughs. 'This is a strictly all-girls' trip. Apart from Brewster, of course. And, young lady, might I remind you that you're only thirteen! Far too young for a serious boyfriend.'

'Worth a try,' I shrug.

'You've made the right decision, Sassy,' Tas says, handing me the phone. 'Now call Megan right away. Before you change your mind.'

So I phone her. And she's delighted. And

strangely enough, when I hear how pleased she is, I'm glad that I overcame the jealousy-monster. After all, it's only for one weekend. And I used to be such good friends with her when we were small. Maybe Taslima and Cordelia are right. Maybe she's OK after all. And maybe being in a group of four friends might work too. Though a friendship rectangle doesn't sound quite as good as a triangle, does it?

By teatime it's all planned. We'll be leaving first thing on Friday morning. Mum has arranged to borrow a camper van from her mad hippy friend, Cathy, so we can all travel together. And what's more, Cathy's van runs on a new bio-fuel made from seaweed, so it's less harmful to the environment than petrol or diesel. Dad will stay at home, run the country from our front room, and look after Houdini.

And next Saturday night, I'll be doing my first ever gig!

17

That night Dad calls me into the living room. He's got his SERIOUS FATHER face on, so I guess what's coming. Sure enough, he sits me down for a lecture.

Apparently, I must behave impeccably at the Wiccaman or I will never ever be allowed to go anywhere again ever in my whole entire life.

'Does that include school?' I ask mischievously. 'And Great-Gran's?'

'Sassy!' Dad snaps. 'I am deadly serious. I was young once upon a time. I know what goes on at these festivals, and they can be very dangerous for young girls.'

'OK! OK!' I giggle. 'Chill, Papa! I was only joking.'

'And I don't want you drinking any alcohol whatsoever. Not even a sip. Do you understand?'

'I promise, Dad, I will not take any alcohol,' I sigh. As if! I hate alcohol anyway. I had a sip of Mum's gin and tonic when I was about four. It was totally disgusting. Like drinking perfume.[13]

'And drugs, Sassy. You must not touch drugs of any sort. Or accept anything from a stranger that looks like a sweetie, because it might not be.'

'Look, Dad,' I explain as patiently as I can. 'I don't eat sweets anyway. They are full of E-numbers, which are, in fact, drugs. And I have absolutely no intention of sniffing or snorting or snorkelling anything dodgy and ending up a saddo singer with a disappearing nostril. Neither do I intend ever falling in and out of taxis drunk, or putting my knickers on show to the general public.'

Dad's mouth falls open. I do not normally say the word 'knickers' in his presence.

He clears his throat noisily. 'Good. Glad to hear it. I'm only warning you for your own good. These music types can be very persuasive.'

'And I am not easily swayed by other people,' I protest. 'I do know my own mind, Dad!'

'Well, that's true,' says Mum, who's just come in and perched on the arm of Dad's chair. 'Remember, Angus, when we were at the seaside that time, and all the other kids were going daft because they were giving out free ice cream. And you told Sassy to go and get a free ice cream too.

[13] Which I did when I was five. And, incidentally, I have since discovered it DOES have alcohol in it!

And Sassy refused. *I don' wan ithe kweam*, she said. *I'm all fulled up.* And you thought she'd regret it and be crying later because she'd missed out. But she didn't.'

Mum looks all dreamy for a moment. Like she always does when she talks about when me and Pip were little. Sometimes she even says they were the best days of her life. Which I do hope they weren't, cos there has to be more to life than constantly chasing around after two snot-nosed, soggy-bottomed weenies.

'OK,' Dad says at last. 'So you do understand, Sassy, that, as MY daughter, I expect you to behave perfectly while you're away?'

I nod.

'Say it out loud, please,' he says sternly. Honestly! When he's not being an MP Dad's a lawyer, and sometimes he forgets I'm his child, not the accused.

I raise my right hand and chant in a monotone. 'I-promise-I-will-behave-myself-and-not-let-any-one-lead-me-astray-and-not-take-any-alcohol-or-drugs-or-speak-to-bad-men-so-help-me –'

'Sassy!' Dad interrupts. 'I hope you're taking this seriously!'

'Of course I'm taking it seriously!' I say in my best most serious voice.

'But we want you to have fun too!' Mum exclaims.

'No, we don't!' Dad objects.

Mum scowls at him. 'Calm down, will you! You have nothing to worry about, Angus. I'm going to be there, keeping a beady eye on her. I don't know what you're stressing about!'

'In that case,' Dad smiles, 'I hope you have a great time.'

I stagger from the living room, feeling like I've just been put through a shredding machine. And I feel guilty! Even though I haven't done anything.

As I crawl upstairs I make a solemn promise to myself. When I have children I will NEVER EVER put them through this. It's quite easy really. It's just my silly parentals who can't seem to get their heads round it.

As a parent, I will simply trust my sproglets.

18

All week, every day after school, I practise my guitar like crazy.

Cos the weather's good and the Wiccaman's an open-air festival, I try rehearsing out in the garden. You know, just to get the feel of it. And can you believe it? Even though my guitar's acoustic – so it's not like it's amplified or anything – our crotchety neighbours complain about the noise pollution! A bit rich considering the horrible stink they kick up when they cook half a cow at a time on their barbecue.

Tas had a tough time convincing her mother to let her come along to the festival. She pointed out how she wouldn't be missing school or anything, but even so Mrs Ankhar wouldn't say yes. In the end, my mum had to phone and be all reassuring about how strict she'd be with us and how she'd not let us near boys or drugs or alcohol. Eventually Mrs Ankhar gave in and Mum sat down for a stiff gin and tonic to recover.

The evening before we leave Mum and Pip go off to Paradiso's (*the superstore that makes shopping heavenly*) to stock up with food and juice for the weekend.

I, of course, refuse to accompany them. Paradiso's are the biggest superstore chain in the country and they still use far too much plastic in their packaging, which, as I have pointed out to the managing director, is hugely damaging to the environment. They stock eggs from factory chickens that have been treated disgracefully, they sell genetically modified food products which will probably cause us all to grow extra thumbs or worse, and they pay their staff peanuts.[14]

'OK, OK, OK!' Mum says, backing out of the door and trailing Pip with her. 'Spare me the politics! We need to eat, Sassy. And food at the festival will cost an arm and a leg. So *you* stay at home, *you* keep your principles intact, and *we'll* get the shopping.'

While they're gone I make the final choice of what I'd like to wear on stage. Last night Cordelia and Taslima – and Megan – came round. They were so-o-o-o excited.

Each of them brought an outfit for me to try. Megan came up with a zingy pink, tight-fitting short dress. Everyone said I looked really cool in

[14] Well, not literally, obviously.

it, and it did make my legs look long, but when I picked up my guitar and strummed it a few times, there was a problem.

'Oh no!' Megan gasped. 'Now it looks like you've no skirt on at all!'

I strummed a few times more and wiggled my hips.

'And now we can see your knickers!' Cordelia dissolved in a puddle of giggles.

'In any case, zingy pink just isn't you, Sass,' Taslima said, wrinkling her nose. 'You're giving out all the wrong kinds of messages. Pink messages.'

'I bet Magnus would love it!' Cordelia stopped giggling just long enough to say. 'Maybe I should phone him!'

'Don't you dare!' I said, tugging the dress off and passing it back to Megan. 'And thanks, Megan. It's a lovely dress, but I don't want to start my career with my knickers on show! It's a bit too Arizona Kelly for me!'

'OK, OK, OK! Try my stuff next,' Cordelia said, drying her eyes and pulling a tiny red-and-purple kilt from her tote bag. 'I'm working on this kind of tartan theme at the moment. You know, kind of Scotty-Dog-Goth.' (Cordelia's stuff is all stunning, and cos she designs and makes it herself, it's totally unique.)

So I stepped into the kilt and pulled on its

matching lacy purple top. Cordelia insisted I also wear purple fishnet tights and black Doc Martens that laced right up to my knees. Then she fastened a little red dog collar studded with diamonds round my neck and a smaller one round each wrist.

I stared in the mirror. I looked like a kid that's been let loose in a fancy-dress shop. It just didn't work. This time it was Megan who fell on the floor, laughing hysterically.

'What I don't understand,' she snorted, 'is how Cordelia looks so fantastic in everything she makes, but no one else can carry it off!'

'I think we instinctively dress the way that suits us,' Taslima said, carefully folding the dress she'd brought along and putting it back into her neat little case. 'And you should wear what you always do, Sass. What you like yourself in. You know, cargo pants or jeans. A vest-top or Tee.'

'I agree,' said Megan. 'The way you dress is the way you are, Sassy. Kinda wild and natural.'

So that's why I'm setting all my trousers and tops out on my bed now, so I can find what I think would look best on stage. In the end I choose a pair of tight blue jeans and a sky-blue vest with fluffy white clouds floating across it. I choose a plain silver chain with a little dolphin charm to wear round my neck. I turn the jeans up to just below the knee. Then I pick up my guitar and pose in front of the mirror. It looks fine. Good enough. And I like the bare feet. Maybe I should always perform in bare feet.

Anyway, I remind myself as I take everything off again and pack it into my overnight bag, it's my singing that counts, not the way I look.

It's almost nine o'clock that night and I'm in the kitchen mooching for something to snaffle, when the doorbell rings.

'I'll get it,' I shout, stuffing a muffin in my mouth, not expecting it to be for me. I open the door and there stands Twig. He smiles shyly and my heart does a back-flip and lands unsteadily.

As we go through to the kitchen, Twig nods at the rucksacks piled high in the hall. 'You've got all your packing done, then?' he asks.

'Yeah, we're off first thing.'

'So you won't have room for anything else?' he smiles through his flop of hair.

'Mum says you can't come. I already asked.'

'That's a shame,' he pulls a sad-clown face. 'But you might have room for this.' And he produces a small bundle from behind his back and holds it out to me.

I open it out. It's a white cotton T-shirt. On the front it says *BOYCOTT PARADISO'S*. I turn it to the back. There's a drawing of the Planet Earth, all beautiful and blue and green like the way it's supposed to look from outer space – but with a huge ugly black insect sitting on top of it, and a big chunk eaten out of it. Above the planet it says *PARADISO'S*. Underneath it says: *ARE PARASITES*.

'It was one of Megan's old ones. So I recycled it,' Twig grins. 'And did the drawings, of course.'

Just then Pip comes clattering downstairs.

'What's a pa-ra-site?' she asks, peering at the Tee Twig's just given me.

'It's an organism that feeds off other living things, gobbles them up and gives nothing in return,' Twig says, but Pip just looks more confused.

'Like when Brewster gets a tick in his fur,' I explain. 'It sucks blood from him and gets big and fat and doesn't do him any good at all.'

'I don't get it,' says Pip. 'How can a superstore be like a tick? One's tiny and the other's huge. Anyway I don't really care.' She flicks her hair and twirls a couple of times. 'Do you like my new dress?'

Twig and I stare as she supermodel-catwalks up and down the kitchen.

'New dress?' I gasp. 'How come *you* got a new dress?'

'Cos *I* went shopping with Mum,' Pip smiles.

'You got it in Paradiso's?' I ask, surprised.

'Yes, we did,' says Mum as she floats through

in her silk dressing gown, her hair piled high on her head and plastered with some sort of weird dark-green paste. 'And, before you ask, it's henna. A natural hair dye. I'll be rinsing it off in a few minutes.'

'But it's GREEN!' I blurt. 'I am not going anywhere with a GREEN mother.'

Mum looks pityingly at me. 'It washes out, silly. And then my hair will be a beautiful rich auburn. You'll see. I used to henna it when I was young.' She pauses to look at the T-shirt Twig has designed.

'*Paradiso's are Parasites,*' she reads. 'So Sassy has brainwashed you too, Twig?'

'Not at all,' says Twig. 'Everyone knows that Paradiso's gets away with murder.'

'With murder?' Mum laughs, filling the kettle to make a cup of tea. 'Isn't that a bit strong?'

Just then Dad comes into the kitchen and Pip tosses her hair and does a few twirls for him.

'Maybe not murder,' Twig concedes. 'But almost as bad. Paradiso's uses little kids in sweatshops to make their clothes. They have to work really long hours in horrible conditions and hardly get paid anything. That's how they keep their prices down.'

'Is what Twig says right, Angus?' Mum asks Dad. 'Do you know anything about this?'

Dad sighs heavily. 'There is evidence. Yes. And your dress is lovely, Pip. Very you.'

'So how come no one told *me*?' Mum continues, indignant.

'Well, I have tried –' I begin, but Mum's not listening.

'Why's it not all over the papers?' she goes on. 'I mean, if **I'd** known I would **NEVER** have bought that dress for Pip! To think that a little kid her age might have had to work long hours to make it! That's dreadful.'

'Paradiso's are so powerful,' Dad sighs. 'They aren't just a supermarket. They own newspapers and TV stations. They control a lot of the media.'

'So how come you two know all about their sweatshops?' Mum asks me and Twig.

'The Internet,' I say.

'Websites like YouSaveTheySlave.com,' Twig adds. 'The info's out there if people want to find it. But, to be honest, most people would rather have their cheap clothes. Not ask too many questions.'

Just then Pip comes back into the kitchen in her pink frilly dressing gown. Solemnly, she hands Mum a Paradiso's bag.

'What's this?' Mum says.

'It's that dress,' Pip says quietly. 'You can take it back to Paradiso's. I don't want it. Not if little kids were forced to make it.'

I stare at Pip. Can this really be my fashion-daft, shopaholic little sis?

Mum gives her a big hug – and almost covers her in green slime from her hair. Pip pushes her away.

'See,' Pip says, smiling at Twig. 'Sassy and you aren't the only ones with princey-thingies around here. I can be an eco-warrior too!'

'And you're the best little sis in the world,' I grin, planting a kiss on her cheek.

'I know,' she says. 'And the prettiest! And now I'm going to bed to get my beauty sleep.'

And with that, and a double twirl, she waves goodnight.

19

Twig and I wander outside to get away from the parentals who are totally clogging up the kitchen. It's dusk and the scent from the roses and honeysuckle by the fence hangs heavy in the air.

We wander to the old swing at the bottom of the garden. I sit down and sway gently backwards and forwards. Twig looks down at me and smiles.

'I love the T-shirt,' I say, trying to sound normal, but feeling all light-headed. 'I'll wear it on stage on Saturday night. It's perfect. It's like I can make a statement, you know, without saying anything.'

'I wish I was going to the festival,' he says quietly.

'I wish you were coming too.' I smile up at him.

'Really?'

'What do you mean – *really*?' I laugh and the sound seems unnaturally loud in the still evening air.

'It's just . . .' he begins, then stops.

'Just what?'

'Well, things are going to change for you. You're going to meet people like Phoenix Macleod . . .' Twig hangs his head and his hair flops over his face.

'So?'

'So you wouldn't want me there, not really,' he mumbles.

I stand up suddenly so my eyes are level with Twig's. He lifts his head and I hold his gaze and the whole world seems to spin.

'I'm not interested in Phoenix Macleod.'

'You're not?'

'I'm not,' I smile. Then add jokingly, 'Anyway, Phoenix Macleod's way too old for me. He's at least fifteen!'

'Megan doesn't think he's too old. He's her ideal guy.'

'But he's not mine . . . And I *do* wish you were coming to the festival.'

Above us the sky's almost dark.

'So are you going to make a wish?' Twig points to a single tiny star twinkling high above the trees.

I love wishing on the first star. When I was little I used to wish for childish things, like a new bike, or a pet rabbit. There are so many important things I could wish for now. Like world peace, or an end to cruelty to animals, or for someone to discover a fuel that doesn't cause global warming, or a miracle cure for cancer.

But I'm not going to wish for any of those. Not this time. Cos there's something I'd like more than anything. Something special just for me.

Twig takes my hand and pulls me towards him, and I'm standing so close I can feel his breath against my cheek.

I look up at the star and make my wish. Silently.

'So what are you wishing for?' Twig whispers.

'Can't tell you,' I say softly, 'or the wish won't come true. And it's too important to spoil it.'

Twig's thoughtful for a moment. 'You didn't wish for a platinum disc or something like that, did you?' he teases.

'Nope,' I reply.

Then we sit together on the picnic table, holding hands, till the sky looks like a blue-black sea with diamonds swirling through it.

'Twig,' I say into the darkness.

'Yeah?' he says softly.

'Are you my boyfriend now?' I ask nervously.

He squints at me through his flop of hair, then looks down at our clasped hands.

'Looks like it,' he smiles. 'Are you my girlfriend?'

'Yeah, I am,' I say, holding up my wrist. 'That's why I'm wearing your friendship bracelet.'

'So I'll see you when you get back from the festival?'

'Yep,' I smile. 'I guess so.'

Just then Mum opens the kitchen door and lets Brewster out for his late-night sniff around the garden.

'I have to go,' Twig says as golden light spills from the open door across the lawn. He stands up and lets go of my hand. 'Be brilliant at the festival.'

'I'll do my best. And I'll wear the T-shirt. For luck.' His face is only inches from mine, and I think he's about to kiss me. Then Mum shouts for Brewster and Twig disappears into the deepening darkness.

I sit on in the garden, rocking slowly backwards and forwards on the swing, gazing up at the sparkling scatter of stars, the lovely milk-white moon.

And I don't mind if the wish I made on the first star doesn't come true right away. Cos Twig's my boyfriend, and I'm his girlfriend. It's all official now.

So it can only be a matter of time until he kisses me . . . can't it?

20

The following morning Mum insists we must drop into Paradiso's on our way to the Wiccaman so she can return Pip's unwanted dress. Otherwise, she reasons, it will be next week before she can take it back, and they might be difficult about giving a refund.

So once we're all piled into the van with our rucksacks and my guitar and Pip's little pink roll-along suitcase and Brewster and his dog bowl, and Dad's been given his final instructions on where to find the stash of extra toilet paper and how to work the microwave and what to feed – and not feed – Houdini, Mum starts up the engine and we go chugging off down the road.

Mum looks stunning, her hennaed hair glowing a rich dark chestnut in the sun. She's not wearing her usual clothes either, but has dug out some old stuff I didn't even know she had. A creamy cheese-cloth blouse with little bells on the cuffs that jangle every time she moves her hands, a long, floaty patchwork skirt, a pair of flat sandals with little diamonds studded in them. *And* she's remembered to put her jewellery on too – bangles and earrings and a necklace. She looks totally mad, but kind of attractive with it.

As always, Paradiso's car park is mobbed. Mum eventually trundles the van into a space and we all tumble out. But then she can't find the bag with Pip's dress, so Cordelia has to climb back inside and psychically detect it. Eventually she finds it under Brewster's bottom. It's a bit crushed – and warm – so Taslima smoothes it out and flaps it in case it smells a bit doggy, then pops it back in the bag and hands it to Mum.

By this time Megan's decided she needs the loo again, even though we all went – on Mum's orders – when we left the house, so we decide to lock the van and while the others go into Paradiso's I'll let Brewster have some fresh air.

While Megan and Cordelia and Taslima head to the toilet, Pip goes with Mum to the Customer Care counter. 'It should only take a minute,' Mum says.

Five minutes later I'm still waiting at the door with Brewster on his lovely new yellow lead.

Five minutes after that Cordelia and Megan and Taslima come back from the loos and join me. Five more minutes pass. Still no sign of Mum or Pip.

'I'm going in to find them,' I say at last. 'Mum's probably decided she needs more shopping.'

And so we all traipse into the store. Only to find Mum still at the Customer Care counter. Looking anything but cared for.

'I think you're being unnecessarily difficult!' Mum says through gritted teeth. (Always a danger sign.) The Customer Care lady puffs herself up inside her uniform and eyes Mum coldly.

'I've explained to you already, Madam,' she says, bundling the dress back into its carrier bag and pushing it across the counter to Mum. 'The labels have been cut off. You have not provided a valid purchase receipt. We cannot give you your money back. And,' she smiles smugly, 'how do we know your little girl hasn't worn it already?'

'Because I've just told you so!' Mum counters, waving her arms in a tinkling of exasperation and tiny bells.

'And you think I should take your word for it?' The Customer Care lady runs a disapproving eye over Mum . . . then Pip . . . then all of us.

'I most certainly do!' Mum retorts. 'And I can't see why not –'

'Well, let's just say we've had some bad experiences with you New Age hippy types before,' the Customer Care lady says sniffily. Then she signals to a big burly security guard in a Paradiso's uniform. 'Bill,' she calls. 'Can you see these people off the premises! And, Madam,' she says to Mum. 'Perhaps you could teach your children to read?' She points to a 'No Dogs' notice on the wall. 'Dogs are *not* allowed in Paradiso's stores. For hygiene reasons.' She adds sniffily, 'But then you types wouldn't know anything about that!'

The security man moves towards us. Mum looks like she's going to swing for the Customer Care lady, and I'm thinking, *well, this is it, the end of Dad's career as a politician*, when Cordelia grabs my arm.

'Do you mind,' she says to the security guard in a really loud voice so everyone around stops and turns. 'Brewster is a BLIND dog. Don't you dare put a finger near him or I'll order him to bite – *and* I'll let the papers know!'

Everyone turns and stares at me and Brewster.

'Here, Sass,' Cordelia says, 'you know you should be wearing your dark glasses when we're out in public.' And she sticks her sunglasses on me.

'What's more,' Pip says to the Customer Care lady, in a clear, sweet voice. 'We are *not* New Age hippies. We are from the Children's Sunshine Home for Sick Kids. That's our van out there in the car park. The one with the rainbows on the side. We painted it ourselves, even though . . .' her voice falters and her chin trembles as she brings her acting skills into play. Cordelia puts a protective arm round her.

'Don't get upset, Tiny Pip,' Cordelia says, 'you know how bad stress is for . . . your condition . . .'

A crowd has formed around us now, all concerned faces and disgusted muttering. Bill, the security guard, looks to the Customer Care lady, unsure what to do. A couple of people have taken out their mobile phones and have started videoing what's going on.

'The girl with the curly hair's blind,' I hear one woman tell a man who's just come over. 'They're trying to throw her out because of her guide dog.'

I stare straight ahead, glad I've got Cordelia's sunglasses on. My heart starts racing and my mouth goes dry. What if someone from school recognizes me? What if they shout, *Hey, Sassy, what are you doing pretending to be blind?*

'So maybe you could just give me my money back and we'll get back to the Home?' Mum says to the manager, who's just arrived, sweating heavily.

'After all,' Megan pipes up. 'I'm sure Paradiso's don't want to be known as the store that threw the blind kid out!'

The muttering from the crowd increases and the manager sweats even more.

Then Taslima takes me firmly by the arm and guides me towards the exit. And all the time I'm trying to stare straight ahead, and my pulse is racing because I'm sure that impersonating a blind person is a really despicable thing to do and if I'm caught I'll probably be put on the Delinquent Child Register, and forever people will point at me and whisper, *yes, that's her . . .*

Taslima is guiding me through the sliding doors when Brewster almost ruins everything by trying to snaffle an ice lolly from a little kid.

'We're still training him,' Megan smiles at the child's mother as Taslima pushes me forward. Then we walk in a silent, dignified huddle until we get into the van, where the others burst into giggles on the floor.

'I don't see what's so funny,' I say. 'I'm traumatized. I'll probably need months of therapy to recover.'

Minutes later, Mum climbs in. 'There you go,' she grins, chucking a big bag of crisps and juice and choccy bars over to us. 'Customer Care wants to apologize – and give the Sick Kids a treat. Now let's get out of here!'

With a jingle of her hippy bracelets she revs the van into life, and we go chugging off, on our way at last to the Wiccaman festival!

21

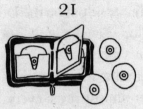

The first part of the journey is all motorway. Pip sits up front beside Mum[15] and after a while we all play a crazy version of I SPY to keep her amused. We've brought CDs with us for the journey, so Pip takes charge of the music. We each get to choose three tracks at a time, and can you believe it, Megan chooses the same Phoenix Macleod track every time! In the end we threaten to stop the van and put her out if she doesn't choose something else. (I have to admit, though, he's pretty awesome.)

At last Mum turns off from the motorway and we bounce our way through rolling countryside. The camper's getting hotter and hotter but when we try to open the windows all but one is jammed shut. To cool us down, Taslima dives over the back and tugs out the picnic bag filled with car-

---

[15] Since the trip to Great-Gran's Mum insists on keeping a beady eye on her.

tons of juice and we all slurp them noisily. Then we raid the bag of goodies from Paradiso's and I chomp my way happily through a bumper bag of Wiggly Worms.

The festival's being held on a farm beside the sea. With only a few miles to go we start seeing more and more signs for it. When we see the first poster advertising Phoenix Macleod, Megan screams and Mum nearly crashes into a tree.

Then everyone starts chattering at once about how exciting it all is. Megan says, 'Oh, I envy you so much, Sassy! You're actually really going to be on stage with Phoenix! Omigod! You're such a lucky duck!'

And I know I'm a lucky duck. But the closer we get to the festival, and the more everyone chatters about how great it's all going to be, the more I realize that I'm going to have to get up on stage in front of hundreds of people. And that's when I start getting this weird tummy ache.

'No wonder your tummy's upset,' Mum says when I complain. 'You've just eaten a full pack of Wiggly Worms!'

'Or maybe it's that tummy bug,' Taslima frowns. 'The one Miss Peabody had.'

'Oh, I hope it's not a tummy bug!' Mum exclaims. 'Or Sassy certainly won't be performing tomorrow night.'

Just then we pass another big Phoenix Macleod poster and Cordelia clasps a hand over Megan's mouth. 'In the interests of Road Safety,' Cordelia grins as Megan squeaks through her clamped fingers.

The poster's huge, with Phoenix smiling cheekily, his dark curls falling down over his coal-black eyes, and across the top it says in huge letters: *PHOENIX MACLEOD WICCAMAN FESTIVAL SATURDAY MAIN STAGE 7.30 p.m.*

'Huh!' Pip puffs indignantly. 'Sassy's name's not even on it!'

'Yeah,' says Megan, pushing Cordelia's hand away good-naturedly. 'But just wait! When Y-Gen sign Sassy her name will be right up there, at the top –'

'And I'll be able to go around saying, *Oh yes, Sassy Wilde? That's my daughter!*' Mum says in a silly posh proud-mother voice.

'And we'll be able to say, *Oh yes, we used to know her!*' Cordelia teases.

'*Before she became too famous for the likes of us!*' Taslima adds.

Everyone's giggling. Having fun. But I'm not laughing. For the first time it's beginning to dawn on me just how much is riding on this gig. If I fail, I won't just be letting myself down. I'll be letting everyone else down too. Suddenly my tummy starts churning like a cement mixer. And I don't think it's got anything to do with tummy bugs. Or Wiggly Worms. It's nerves!

Pip looks over her shoulder at me. 'Don't look so worried,' she smiles. 'I know being a star won't change you at all. You'll always be my horrible big sister!'

Just then an alarm sounds and the engine chugs dramatically. Mum swerves on to the grass verge as a puff of green smoke billows out from under the bonnet.

'Oh dear!' Quickly, she switches the engine off. With a dramatic wail the high-pitched screech of the alarm eventually fades into silence. 'Cathy said there might be some problem with the bio-fuel,' Mum mutters apologetically. 'I guess this is what she meant. She said to wait ten minutes till it cools down.'

We sit in silence, watching the van's little clock tick-tock slowly forward. Mum says we have to stay in the van because of all the traffic whizzing past, so we sweat it out, the sun cooking us pink, till the engine's temperature cools.

'Does anyone smell fish?' Taslima screws her nose up as Mum starts the engine again.

'The bio-fuel's made from seaweed,' Mum explains. My tummy lurches alarmingly. Cordelia, psychic as always, shoves me towards the open window. Gratefully, I stick my head out and gulp in big lungfuls of country air.

'I guess this is what a sardine feels like,' Taslima yawns, as we trundle the last few miles. 'You know, locked inside a tin stinking of fish.'

By the time we get to the Wiccaman farm we're all hot and bothered. Mum follows the little signposts till we find the 'Yurt Village' on the edge of a small wood.

'I think this is us, girls!' Mum announces as we at last pull up at Yurt No. 3.

We all cheer and tumble out.

Cordelia and Pip and Megan and Taslima go dashing straight into the yurt to give it the once-over. Mum sticks her head under the bonnet and peers helplessly at the green smoke which is once again pouring from Cathy's bio-ethanol engine.

And me? I make a dash for the nearest toilet, hoping that it really is just the Wiggly Worms that have upset my tummy.

22

The yurt is brilliant!

It's like this mad sort of tent thing. But though it's covered in canvas it's got a real wooden door, and inside there are brightly patterned woven rugs on the floor and all these lovely low sofas with throws over them, and huge embroidered cushions in dark greens and rich blues and deep blood reds.

'It's like something from the *Arabian Nights*!' Taslima sighs happily as she drapes herself across one of the sofas, her dark skin and huge brown eyes making her look like an exotic Eastern princess. 'Bring me my Turkish Delight!' she purrs sexily, and we all giggle. It is such a non-Taslima thing to do!

'The sofas double as beds,' Megan reads from the *Advice to First-Time Yurters* booklet she's picked up off the coffee table. 'And you can roll up the canvas sides to let more light and air in.'

So we set about rolling the sides up. And that's

when I see Mum. And she's not alone. There's a man looking under her bonnet!

I zoom outside.

'I've never seen one of these before,' the man's saying in a deep gravelly voice. 'I'm more a bike man myself.' He nods his mop of greying hair at a huge shiny motorbike sitting in the sunshine, gleaming, outside one of the other yurts. 'But I'll take a look at it if you want, er . . .'

Mum flashes him a huge smile. 'Heather,' she says.

'Heather,' the biker repeats like he's never heard the name before. 'Heather.' And he stands staring at Mum like some kind of lovesick puppy!

Something has to be done! I've seen enough soaps to know that my mother's at a very danger-ous age. And she's just finished her *Release Your Inner Wild Woman* self-help book. I grab Brewster's dog basket from the back of the van.

'Mum!' I say sharply. 'Where should I put this?'

'On the floor, honey?' Mum says with a dreamy shake of her copper curls.

'Excuse me,' I say, pushing the Lovesick Biker aside and plonking the dog basket where he was standing moments before. 'Busy, busy, busy!'

'Sassy!' Mum exclaims. 'I meant INSIDE the yurt! Can't you see I'm talking to . . . I'm sorry, I don't know your name.' She holds out her hand in a jingle of bracelets.

'Kris,' he says, taking her hand and holding it for what, I feel, is longer than is strictly necessary. 'Kris with a K.'

And I'm just thinking about slamming the bonnet of the van down on Kris-with-a-K's other hand – even though I feel it would be an act of violence and I am not a violent person – when there's a blood-curdling yowl from inside our yurt and Pip comes running out.

'Looks like you've got your hands full,' Kris-with-a-K grins. 'Maybe we could have a drink when the kids are in bed.'

'She doesn't drink,' I say quietly to Kris-with-a-K as Mum makes off with Pip clamped to her leg. 'My father forbids it.'

Kris-with-a-K raises an eyebrow.

'It doesn't agree with her medication,' I continue. 'She's not long out of rehab.'

'Thanks for letting me know, kid,' Kris-with-a-K says, looking at Mum with what I like to think is a fresh perspective, as Pip drags her into the yurt. 'Poor woman. I'll see if I can fix her engine anyway.'

Happy that I have cooled his ardour towards my mother and saved my parents' marriage, I carry Brewster's basket into the yurt and plonk it down.

'We can't stay here!' Pip is whining. 'I can't find a mirror. Anywhere! *And* there's no bathroom scales!'

'Pip!' Mum scolds. 'This is a yurt. It's like camping. If you must have a mirror, you can use the little one in the van. And what on earth do you need bathroom scales for?'

'In case I put weight on,' Pip says, pouting.

'That's so ridiculous, Pip!' I exclaim. 'You are such a skinny little minny. You NEED to put weight on!'

'You're perfect as you are, sweetie,' Mum says, giving her a hug. 'So no more of this fretting about how you look. You're nine years old. You should be running about enjoying yourself.'

Just then Megan, Cordelia and Taslima come running in. Like nine-year-olds.

'We found the beach!' Cordelia whoops. 'The water looks gorgeous! Can we go swimming, please, Heather?' She turns her wide green eyes on Mum.

'That's a great idea!' Mum smiles. 'Go and cool down after that long hot drive. It will give me a chance to get this place organized. But first, Sassy, you have to take Brewster for a walk.'

'Why me?' I protest.

'Because it will keep you grounded.' Mum answers. 'We don't want you getting above yourself, do we? None of this star nonsense. Anyway, I'm worried about Brewster. I think the journey in the van's upset his digestive system. You know how delicate he is.'

'What about *my* digestive system?' I mutter.

Honestly, my mum worries more about the dog than me!

'He's not performed all day,' Mum continues, totally ignoring me. She clips on Brewster's lead and thrusts a poop-scoop bag into my hand. 'So don't come back till he's done.'

I do wish Mum could find a different verb to describe Brewster's toilet needs. I like to think of 'performing' as a high art, something of merit, something we 'performers' do.

'OK,' I sigh. 'Come on, boy. There's a lovely wood behind the yurt. Lots of trees. You'll have a ball.'

'We'll come with you if you want,' Taslima says kindly. But Megan and Cordelia are already halfway into their swimming togs.

I shake my head. 'No, it's fine. You go ahead. I'll meet you down there.'

'Are you sure?' Megan asks. 'Because we could get dressed again and come with you.' And I don't know why, but when Megan says something kind and considerate I'm still not convinced she's sincere. Maybe it's me that's the problem. Maybe I just find it difficult to trust her cos she used to tell such whopping great lies.

'Thanks, Megan,' I say quickly. 'That's really kind. But I'll be fine. Honest.'

And then my buds head off in a colourful rush of flapping towels and high-pitched giggling. The yurt falls silent and Brewster looks at me with sad, unseeing eyes. The thing is, Brewster's pretty old. Fifteen, in fact. Which in Doggy Years makes him one hundred and five, so I'm not surprised his digestive system's been traumatized by a long journey in a van stinking of fish and full of over-excited girls.

'Don't come back until he's done something!' Mum warns as she shoos me out of the door and gives a little wave to Kris-with-a-K who's got half the camper van engine strewn about the grass now.

I wander aimlessly through the sun-dappled wood. I look up through the branches at the green and blue mosaic of tree and sky. Woods make me think of Twig. Right at this moment I'd give any-thing to be hit on the head by a nut. (As long as Twig was chucking it, of course.)

At first Brewster sniffs every tree we pass. He tries to raise his leg from time to time, but keeps falling over.[16] As we wander through the sun-dappled shadows I send him thought waves to try to make his digestive system work faster, but all he does is tug at some grass and chew it.

By the time we reach the other side of the wood he still hasn't, errr . . . performed. From here I can see the stage and I watch, fascinated, as the techies

[16] And Great-Gran thinks she's got problems! She should try being an elderly dog for a while.

and roadies get everything ready. One guy with dreadlocks, perched on the light rigging high above the stage, clips spotlights under its curved roof. Another, a tall skinny fellow in tight black jeans, fiddles with a mike. Every so often he says ONE TWO ONE TWO. His voice booms and screeches as a totally bald guy adjusts the settings at a soundboard at the side of the stage.

I watch, mesmerized. *Am I really going to go out there tomorrow night, just me and my guitar?*

I try to imagine what it will be like when the whole field is filled with people, all looking towards the stage, and I feel my blood pressure shoot up as fast as Swotty Sewell's hand in chemistry. Suddenly all these nightmare scenarios start racing through my head, like what if all my guitar strings break at once, or I lose my voice, or the mike explodes! I'm so caught up in my own private bubble of terror it takes me a few minutes to realize Brewster is tugging on the lead. And then, right there, in front of the main stage, he squats!

I wait for him to finish, trying to pretend he's not with me. Pretty stupid, I know, given I'm holding his lead. At last he stands up and kicks at the grass with his hind legs. What he has deposited is not a pretty sight. And the pong is totally disgusting. His tummy certainly has been unsettled by the journey! I whip the poop-scoop bag from my pocket and, trying not to gag, do my best to scoop the poop.

And that's when I realize I'm not alone. There's a boy watching me. On the grass by the edge of the stage. My heart sinks. Because it's not just any boy. It's Phoenix Macleod.

Quickly, I shove my hand with the poop bag behind my back, then tug Brewster's lead to drag him away from the scene of his crime. But what does the daft mutt do? Only plops his backside down on the grass and starts bottom-walking! You know that thing dogs do when they've got an . . . em . . . personal itch.

'How old is he?' Phoenix asks, walking towards me. I stare at him. He's even better-looking than in his photos! His eyes are dark and thick-lashed, his black hair falls in glossy curls over his forehead. 'Your dog?' Phoenix prompts, bending down and tickling Brewster's ears. 'How old is he?'

'Oh, he's fifteen,' I stammer, desperately trying to keep the poop bag hidden.

Phoenix smiles up at me. 'Same as me,' he says.

Just then one of the roadies waves to Phoenix that he's needed up on stage.

'Looks like I'll have to go,' he grins. 'See you around!' With that he wanders over to the stage and I'm left gripping my bag of stinky poo, staring at the most stunning chico I have ever seen in my entire life!

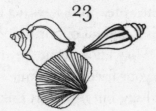

23

By the time I drag Brewster back to the yurt, *and* wash my hands, *and* get changed into my bikini, *and* find a decent towel, Ben and Zing have arrived.

'Enjoying the beach, then?' Ben asks when he sees me in my swim-things. 'It's brilliant, isn't it? We went for a dip earlier.'

Before I can say that I've not actually got as far as the beach yet, Zing pulls a sheet of paper from her bag and hands it to me. 'This will only take a few minutes,' she grins. 'Then your time's your own.'

'Until tomorrow, that is,' Ben chuckles. 'We have big plans for you.'

I stare at the sheet. It's a timetable. Zing passes another copy to Mum.

'So,' says Zing brightly, 'let's just see what's planned. Today's Friday. Tonight's the opening night and of course, Sassy, you're free to go along and enjoy that. Tomorrow, though, we have a big day planned –'

'But I really was hoping to hang out with my friends tomorrow!' I splutter.

Mum shushes me. 'You have to listen to Ben and Zing. This is a great opportunity. They're the professionals. They know what they're doing. You can play with your friends any time.'

'OK, OK!' I say, but my heart sinks. Right now my two bezzies are down at the beach having a ball, and they probably won't be missing me at all. Which hurts more than just a little.

Zing pulls some glossy sheets of paper from her briefcase. 'Yeah,' Zing says. 'We got this fantastic opportunity from *Tween Qween Magazine* for Sassy to do a fashion photo shoot, you know, using the festival as a backdrop –'

'But I don't want to do a fashion shoot!' I gasp. 'I don't want to be a model!'

'But I do,' Pip pipes up. She turns her best smile on Zing and Ben and twirls a few times.

'Your little sis has a good attitude,' Ben grins at me. 'But you've misunderstood, kiddo. We're not trying to turn you into a model, we're trying to get you publicity, get you noticed. Think about it. Record companies pay a fortune to buy ads in magazines. So when Zing found out that *Tween Qween Magazine* was looking for a thirteen-year-old –'

'– I immediately thought of you, Sassy! You're perfect,' Zing enthuses, scattering photos of cool-looking Tees and tops and jeans and shorts on the coffee table.

'What's more,' Zing continues, 'this is right up your street. The clothes are part of an eco-friendly fashion range, all made from pure 100 per cent organic cotton. Let's see.' She rummages through some of the papers in her lap. 'The range is called LOVE YOUR PLANET, and 10 per cent of all profits will go to charities like Protect the Polar Bear –'

'This sounds perfect!' Mum says, flicking through the photos. 'I mean, it does seem to tie in beautifully with what you're about, Sassy.'

'If Sassy doesn't want to, I'll do it!' Pip exclaims. Then she fixes Ben with a serious look. 'Is there a fee?'

'Well, actually, yes,' Ben laughs. 'But we thought, for publicity reasons, that instead of taking the fee for the modelling contract Sassy might want to –'

I brighten suddenly. I can see where Ben is going. I don't want to be a model, and I don't care at all about getting money for myself, but there is something I desperately need some dosh for.

'OK,' I say, excited now. 'I'll do it. So long as whatever money I get paid goes straight to Agnes.'

'Agnes?' Zing asks, puzzled.

'My adopted donkey,' I explain. 'She's spend-ing her twilight years in the Dorset Donkey

Sanctuary. I've pledged to send a fiver every month, and let's just say –' I throw Mum a meaningful look, which, I'm afraid, is lost on her – 'I've been finding it a bit hard.'

Ben chucks his head back and laughs. 'OK, Sassy. Do the photo shoot and we guarantee that Agnes will spend the rest of her days in donkey luxury.'

'Great!' Zing beams. 'So that's sorted. As you can see from the timetable the photo shoot starts at one, so we'll come for you at eleven and take you to our trailer in the performers' enclosure –'

'Ooooh,' Pip squeals, 'is that where Phoenix Macleod's staying?'

Zing smiles. 'Well, yes, but he'll be in a different trailer from Sassy, obviously.'

My heart skips a beat at the mention of Phoenix's name. I don't want it to, but it does.

'So, as I was saying, we'll take you to the trailer,' Zing continues, 'then Chantelle, the make-up artist will do your hair and make-up –' I open my mouth to explain that I'd rather not wear make-up, but Zing raises a hand to silence me. 'Chill, Sassy. We don't want to *change* the way you look. We love it! It's so fresh and natural, and well, different. But everyone needs a little help in front of the cameras. We know what we're doing. So we'll pick you up at eleven, OK?'

'Sure,' I say. 'That all sounds cool.' To be

honest, I'm hot and sticky. Outside the sun is shining and the sky's a brilliant blue, and more than anything I want to get down to the beach before Cordelia and Taslima forget I exist and Megan slots herself neatly into my place in the friendship triangle.

Zing runs through the rest of the timetable. 'The photo shoot should be finished by three, then it's back to the trailer. We'll sort out your set, you know, the songs you're going to sing, then maybe grab a bite to eat.'

'After that,' Ben says, 'we want you to rest for a couple of hours. There's a room for you in the trailer. Then it's a shower, make-up again and straight over to the main stage.'

'So, does that sound OK?' Zing asks as she stuffs all the photos back into her bag. Zing always has a huge bag with her, overflowing with papers. She sees me looking at it. 'It's my portable office,' she jokes. 'I operate a very advanced filing system.'

'Yeah,' Ben teases. 'It's called "Chaos". Zing hasn't joined the laptop age yet.'

'See you tomorrow, then,' Zing says. She gives Ben a playful push, and I realize I'm lucky to be working with Ben and Zing. They're such fun to be around.

At the door Ben turns. 'Trust us, kiddo. We know what we're doing.'

'Yeah, making stars is our business.' Zing gives

me a hug. 'And I've got good vibes about you, Sassy.'

Then they're gone and I grab my towel to head out to the beach at last, when Cordelia and Taslima and Megan come bundling in, their hair wet, their faces sun-reddened and gleaming.

'Oh,' says Megan, throwing herself on to one of the sofas, 'the beach was brilliant, Sass. Why didn't you come?'

24

All afternoon people have been arriving at the festival. While Mum makes the tea she sends us off exploring. Cars and motorbikes and vans and campers are slowly bumping their way along the farm tracks to the camping fields, where a village of blue, green and orange tents is springing up.

They've set up stalls too. Wild-looking people with colourful clothes and long untidy hair and earrings and studs and sun-browned skin. Some stalls are laden with handmade jewellery, while others display candles and incense sticks, handmade cotton dresses and wind chimes. Still others offer body-painting, tattoos, piercings. Most of the stall-holders seem to know each other and everybody's smiling and hugging and good-natured in the sunshine. In the distance we can see the main stage.

'Omigod! Isn't that scary?' Megan gasps, linking arms with me. 'Just think, Sassy, tomorrow night you'll be up there, performing, in front of hundreds of people!'

My tummy wobbles dangerously, but I don't want to let anyone know. Somehow I feel that would make it even harder to keep my nerve. 'No sweat!' I lie. 'It's cool.'

'You are so lucky!' Megan continues. 'If it was me I'd be worried sick about all the things that could go wrong.'

'But nothing will go wrong,' I lie again, trying to suppress all the horrendous scenarios I've been secretly worrying about. I pick up a pale-blue, egg-shaped stone from a 'healing crystals' stall. The label says it's angelite and it has calming properties. 'Don't you think this is the most beautiful colour?' I say, hoping to change the subject.

'But just think,' Megan continues, 'the mike could blow up, or . . . or . . . you could just lose your nerve at the last minute, or totally forget how to play your guitar . . . or . . . you might even trip up as you cross the stage!'

'Honestly, Megan!' I blurt. 'Anyone would think you were *trying* to make me nervous! Pleasepleaseplease stop talking about what could go wrong, will you?'

Megan drops her arm from mine. Her face collapses and for a moment it looks like she's going to burst into tears.

Cordelia quickly links arms with me and Megan. 'Oh come on, you two,' she says brightly. 'Nothing bad's going to happen on stage. I cast an extra-special spell last night to make sure it will all be awesome –'

'Oh no!' Taslima laughs, trying to lighten the mood. 'Last year you cast an extra-special spell to pass your maths – and they lost your test paper!'

'Yeah, so maybe I DID pass!' Cordelia giggles. 'It's just we'll never know. Anyway, no way would I mess things up for you, Sass.'

'Thanks, Cordelia,' I say shakily. 'Whatever happens once I go out on stage, I'll just have to cope. I mean, that's what this gig's all about. Ben and Zing want to see if I can sing in front of a crowd. If I've got what it takes.'

'And you have, Sassy. In bucket-loads!' Taslima puts an arm round my shoulder. 'So there's nothing to worry about, is there?'

Silently, secretly, I cross my fingers.

I so hope Taslima's right.

When we get back to the tent Mum has a lovely big dish of pasta ready for us, with a super tomato sauce and tons of grated cheese on top, and tasty side dishes of chopped cucumber and apple. We gobble it down, then all muck in with the washing up.

'OK!' Mum says when the last pan is finally dripping on the draining board in the little kitchen area. 'No more Cinderellas in my yurt! Off you go and make yourselves beautiful. I want nothing but princesses with me tonight!'

Cordelia dresses up in her complete Scotty Goth look. A red vest-top with black lacy sleeves, a tiny tartan kilt, black fishnet tights and Rocket Dog boots with tartan laces.

Then she sits on a log outside the yurt and patiently paints each of her fingernails a different colour: red, purple, green, black and yellow. In the camper she puts purple eyeshadow on her eyes and outlines them with smudgy black liner. She pulls her long black straight hair up in high bunches and ties them with two big floppy tartan ribbons. Finally, she puts on her diamanté dog-collar choker and wristbands – and looks fantastic! In a weird, tartan, Cordelia sort of way.

Taslima is browner than ever after being down at the beach. She and Megan take ages riffling through the piles of tops and skirts and jeans and shorts Megan's brought.[17] In the end Taslima chooses a little lemon crop-top with pretty straps that really shows off her cappuccino complexion.

'You don't think this top's too . . . er . . . revealing?' Taslima says doubtfully as she teams it with a pair of cut-off jeans and flip-flops.

'Not at all!' Mum reassures her. 'You've such gorgeous skin, Taslima. You look lovely.'

[17] In TWO suitcases! For ONE weekend.

Taslima smiles gratefully. Mrs Ankhar would have a fit if she thought Taslima was going out in anything other than a sensible Tee or polo shirt.

Megan insists on wearing a white miniskirt, even though Taslima points out it will probably get all grass-stained. Then she tries on about ten different tops before she chooses a tight low-cut look-at-me one. When she at last emerges from the yurt Mum does a double take.

'Oh, Megan, that top's lovely but . . . emm . . . maybe it's a bit on the scanty side?' Mum stammers. Megan's face falls and Mum adds quickly, 'Tell you what, take a cardie. A big cardie. In case you get a bit chilled. It'll probably get quite cool when the sun goes down.'

And me? I think about wearing the T-shirt Twig gave me. You know, the *Paradiso's are Parasites* one. I'd like to wear it cos it makes Twig seem closer. In the end, though, I decide against it, cos I've promised I'll wear it on stage tomorrow night, and knowing my luck I might spill juice down it, or accidentally squirt it with tomato ketchup, or get a nose bleed and splatter it with blood. So I leave it safely in my rucksack and go for a vest-top and jeans.

Pip, on Taslima's advice – thank goodness she listens to someone! – puts on a really cute turquoise top with a glitter star on the front, and a sugar-pink frou-frou skirt with lemon leggings. Megan has braided her hair with beautiful yellow ribbons and Cordelia has face-painted a big sunflower on one of her cheeks. She looks incredibly pretty. Like an exotic flower. Or a delicate ballerina doll, the kind you get in a music box.

'OK, my princesses!' Mum says at last. 'Everyone ready?'

We all nod, grinning. It's a gorgeous evening, the heat of the day lingering, the sky cloudless, the sun a huge red ball of fire slowly sinking behind the distant mountains, streaking the sky turquoise, pink, lemon, apricot. The smell of wood fires scents the air. Already we can hear the music from the warm-up band floating across the fields.

I pop Brewster into the back of the van, check that the window's open, and give him a bowl of water and some doggy chews. Kris-with-a-K wolf-whistles softly when Mum emerges from the yurt and I fire him a warning look.

'Have you phoned Dad yet?' I ask Mum, loud enough for Kris-with-a-K to hear.

'Didn't have to,' Mum says quietly as Taslima and Megan go on ahead, Pip dancing happily between them. 'He phoned me. Got a bit of a crisis on his hands.'

'Crisis?' I ask, curious. Since Dad became an MP, i.e., one of those we trust to run our country, there have been several crises.[18] 'But we've only been gone eight hours,' I gasp, checking my watch. 'What is it *this* time?'

'Don't tell Pip,' Mum whispers in my ear, 'but Houdini's on the run again.'

[18] A toilet-roll shortage at the Old Folks' Home, a pig on the run in the town centre and a missing bike at the police station.

25

The opening concert is amazing!

As well as the band there's a fire-eater and a juggler and man and woman on stilts. It's like this weird alternative universe where you can be as outrageous as you want, and everyone's friendly and laughing. But Mum warns us not to get too carried away with the party atmosphere and to stick together.

'Where any big group of people are gathered in one place, girls,' she says solemnly, 'there's bound to be a few weirdos.'

Yeah, I think. *And that Kris-with-a-K is one of them!* Dad should have given *Mum* a pep talk before we left. She's much more at risk than I am. She has far too trusting a nature.

We've all been dancing for a while and waving our hands in the air when I realize that the sun has disappeared completely. It's totally dark, except for the stage lights, all different colours, constantly changing against the pitch black of the mountains behind. It looks quite magical. I gaze at the performers on the stage, playing their guitars and strutting their stuff, and it's really hard to believe that tomorrow night I'll be up there and everyone will be listening to me.

And I'm just starting to freak out, my heartbeat racing and my palms going all sweaty, when someone taps me on the shoulder. I jump about twelve feet in the air.

'Sorry!' Phoenix Macleod shouts in my ear. 'I didn't mean to startle you. They're pretty good, aren't they?' He nods to the band on stage, then takes a swig from a bottle of Hi-Vi.[19]

'Yeah!' I nod. 'Cool!' Cos I can't think of anything more intelligent to say.

'So where's your dog?' Phoenix asks. 'The one who's the same age as me?'

Megan and Cordelia and Taslima are staring at me, pop-eyed. I didn't tell them about meeting Phoenix. I mean, it was all so embarrassing, what with Brewster's poo and all.

'He's in the van. Back at the yurt.' I say hurriedly. 'He can't take the noise.'[20]

'Can't blame him,' Phoenix smiles, leaning in

---

[19] Only the coolest drink in the universe! Fresh-fruit smoothie in recyclable bottles!

[20] Oh no! There I go again. Words of one syllable! He'll think I'm a moron.

close so I can hear him over the sound of the band. 'Has his stomach settled down now?'

I feel my colour rise, and I'm so glad it's dark. Phoenix is so close I'm worried he'll be able to feel the heat radiating from my face. Just then someone tugs at my arm.

'Aren't you going to introduce us?' Megan hollers, fluttering her lashes.

I do all the introductions, and Phoenix shouts, 'OK, so you're Cordelia, you're Megan, you're Taslima.' Then, just as the music dies down at the end of the song, he turns to me and says in a quieter voice, 'And I know who you are.'

'You do?' I stammer.

'Zing told me. She's over there.' He points through the crowd and Zing waves happily and gives us a thumbs up. 'So I thought I'd say hi . . . You're doing the gig with me tomorrow night, aren't you?'

I nod. He takes a mouthful from his bottle of Hi-Vi.

'Want some?' he says. 'It's good for you. Honest. Zing and Ben would never let me have anything else.'

I can hardly refuse, can I? So I take the bottle and sip, terrified I'm going to choke and snort it down my nose like I did once before when I was a bit over-excited. But it goes down fine and I pass the bottle back. Phoenix hands it round the others. Cordelia and Taslima take tiny polite sips and pass it on to Megan. Megan takes a mouthful, then another, then another, then just stands, staring at Phoenix, dreamily clasping the bottle.

'You can keep it if you want,' Phoenix teases, and Megan thrusts it clumsily towards him, spluttering an apology.

Phoenix grins at me as he turns to leave. 'See you at the gig tomorrow, then. If not before.' Then he wanders back through the crowds towards Zing.

Cordelia and Taslima and Megan all ask me questions at once. I try to act cool, but secretly I'm pretty chuffed. I may have missed out on the beach, but I did get to meet Phoenix Macleod. We move a bit further away from the music so we can talk. I tell them all about how sweet he was with Brewster, but don't tell them about the dog-poo fiasco. That would have spoiled the glamour of the story more than just a bit.

Then the music stops and everyone moves to another field to see the big Wiccaman bonfire. Soon it's blazing and crackling and everyone is ooh-ing and aahh-ing. Then there's a fantastic fireworks display and we watch in wonder as rockets whoosh up into the sky and explode high above us with rainbow colours.

'Mu-u-u-m,' Pip whimpers, and wilts suddenly like a little flower that desperately needs water. 'I'm tired.'

Mum heaves Pip up in her arms and insists we all

go back to the yurt. By that point I'm pretty tired too, so I don't really mind, but Megan pouts a bit.

'Tell you what,' Mum says as Pip leans sleepily against her shoulder. 'If we all go back now you can light a campfire. I'll put Pip to bed and you can roast marshmallows.'

With Cordelia's help[21] Mum has the campfire lit in no time at all. Taslima, Megan and I bring out some mats and blankets and cushions from the yurt. Then we light some tea-light candles in little glass yogurt jars Mum cleverly brought from home especially for the purpose, and dot them around. It looks totally magical. As we settle around the brightly crackling fire, we can still hear bands playing.

'If we gobble much more of these,' Taslima says solemnly with a half-chewed blackjack stuck on the end of her finger – what's left of the sweets from Paradiso's – 'we'll end up being REAL sick kids.' And we all laugh.

While we pig out we talk – about Phoenix Macleod.

'I think he's really hot,' Megan says, lolling lazily on to her back and staring dreamily up at the starry sky.

Taslima laughs. 'Yeah, Megan. But you think *all* boys are hot.'

[21] A firelighter and twenty matches.

'Not true,' Megan protests. 'I don't think Twig is, do I?'

'Just as well,' Cordelia squeals, her face eerily lit by the flickering flames of the campfire. 'I mean, he's your stepbro. Isn't that illegal?'

'I like him too,' Taslima says suddenly.

'You like *Twig*?' I say, alarmed.

'Course not.' Taslima chucks a cushion at me. 'Phoenix Macleod, silly!'

'Wow!' Cordelia breathes. 'Taslima Ankhar, that is the first time I have EVER heard you say you fancy a chico.'

'I'm NOT saying I fancy him!' Taslima protests.

'So?' Megan says, rolling on to her tummy and looking straight at Taslima. 'What are you saying?' Her eyes glitter in the firelight.

'All I'm saying,' Taslima says slowly, obviously trying to lie and failing spectacularly, 'is . . . he's . . . well . . . attractive . . .'

'So you DO fancy him!' Cordelia whoops. 'I mean, that's exactly the same thing. It's just another way of saying it.'

Taslima looks to me for help.

'I think Cordelia's right, Tas,' I yawn. 'It's nothing to be ashamed of. Maybe you got a whiff of his fairy-gnomes.'

'Of his WHAT?' Megan squeaks, and it's so obvious she thinks it's something rude!

'Phero-mones,' Taslima explains patiently. 'An

invisible smell that animals and humans emit to attract a mate. And no, Sassy, I'm quite sure I did NOT get a whiff of his pheromones. I just think he seems like a nice boy.'

This sets Cordelia into a fit of giggles. Until she's laughing so much she coughs up a half-chewed midget gem.

Then Taslima exclaims. 'But, Sassy, you had a drink from his Hi-Vi, didn't you?'

'Uh-oh!' says Cordelia. 'Maybe you're the one who got a whiff of his pheromones!'

'That would be so-o-o-o cool!' Cordelia gasps. 'Celebrity Lovers! You'd probably be all over *Hiya!* mag. And you could have a fairy-tale wedding, Sass. Can I be bridesmaid? I'd need to wear black, of course.'

'I do NOT fancy Phoenix Macleod!' I protest, and chuck a cushion at Cordelia. Then everyone chucks cushions at me. 'And anyway,' I gasp, 'didn't we *all* take a swig from his bottle?'

'Oh no!' Cordelia laughs. 'That means we've all had a whiff of his fairy-gnomes!'

'Well, he can't marry us all,' Taslima says. 'That would be polygamy. It's illegal in the UK.'

We stop throwing cushions to think about this for a minute. The fire crackles and hisses, its bright flames licking the darkness.

'So I wonder which one he'll choose, then?' Cordelia says thoughtfully.

'I bet it will be you, Cordelia,' Taslima says. 'You two would look gorgeous together with your jet-black hair.'

Megan pokes at the fire with a long stick and tiny angry sparks burst up into the air.

'In that case,' Cordelia says, plumping a pillow up under her head, 'he's going to be bitterly disappointed. Cos I'm not getting married.'

'What? Never?' says Taslima, pulling her sleeping bag up around her ears.

'Never,' Cordelia yawns.

Just then Mum comes back from the toilets in her long silk dressing gown. I glance across at Kris-with-a-K's yurt, but thankfully it's in darkness. He must have taken the hint.

'OK, girls! Time to get ready for bed!' Mum says softly.

Soon we're all settled down inside. I lie and listen to the murmur of voices from the other yurts, the occasional strum of a sleepy guitar in the distance, the breeze rustling the leaves of the nearby trees. I try my hardest, I really do, to think about Twig. I want his face to be the last thing I see before I drift off into sleep.

But try as I might, another face, with dark curls and coal-black eyes, keeps appearing instead.

26

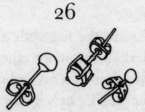

That night I have a dream.

I'm on the big main stage. Singing. The crowd's loving me. They're cheering and whooping and hollering. Taslima and Cordelia and Megan are right down at the front, grinning up at me, and I'm rocking it, singing my heart out.

Then Phoenix comes on stage and the crowd goes wild. We start doing a love duet together. It's my song, 'Pinch Me, I Must Be Dreaming'.

Suddenly I realize something's wrong. The crowd have started to point and laugh.

I look down and see why.

I'm naked. I've got absolutely no clothes on! Not a stitch. I run from the stage. Humiliated.

I wake up. I'm in the yurt. It's not dark any more. Taslima is standing above me, looking down, a puzzled expression on her face.

While everyone else sleeps on, Taslima and I slip out and take Brewster for an early morning walk in the woods. I tell her all about my dream. She listens carefully.

'I don't think it's anything to worry about. It's pretty much standard anxiety stuff,' she explains. 'It's not about clothes. Not about nakedness of the body.' We wait while Brewster sniffs a tree, then tries to pee without falling over.

'You're worried that you're not the real thing and that people will literally "see through" you when you go on stage,' Taslima continues. 'Everyone who performs gets that at some point.' She makes a note in her pink notebook. I try to peer over her shoulder to see what she's written, but she snaps it shut.

'Do you mind? That's confidential! See, it says so there.' She points to the writing on the cover: ***The Crazy Wildes – A Case Study* KEEP OUT!**

'But surely I should be allowed to read the bit about me!' I plead as we gently lead Brewster back towards the yurt. (To be honest I don't want to read the sections on Mum, Dad and Pip. I'm sure they would be way too disturbing.)

'Look,' says Taslima primly, 'I'm the psychologist. I've got to be allowed to make my observations without worrying about how you might react to them. And don't even think about trying to peek!' She tucks the notebook into the back pocket of her shorts. 'You could do yourself untold psychological damage!'

* * *

By the time we get back everyone else is up. Mum's made us each a bowl of yogurt with fresh raspberries on top. She orders us out into the sunshine to eat. All of us, that is, except Cordelia, who has to stay in the shade in case her white skin tans and ruins her Scotty Goth look.

Once we're all dressed and have tidied up our sleeping bags, we go wandering round the stalls. I did want to go for a swim first thing, but Mum wouldn't let me in case I caught cold or got a sore throat. And after my anxiety dream last night I'm not taking any chances.

At the stalls Cordelia buys some earrings for her mum. They're made from tiny pearly seashells threaded together with silver string. Taslima finds a little carved wooden box she thinks Mrs Ankhar would like. And Megan drags us over to look at a stall offering tattoos and body piercings.

'I've always wanted a nose stud,' she whispers, out of earshot of Mum. But Megan hasn't counted on my mother's super-power ability to hear things she shouldn't.

Sure enough, Mum flies over in a flurry of flowery skirt. 'No, Megan. Don't even ask!' she exclaims.

'But it's OK, honest,' Megan says. 'Mum's always said I can have a nose stud if I want. She's cool about body piercings. She's even got some herself.'

'Megan!' Mum says, a note of exasperation in her voice. 'Your mother has her ears pierced. Not her tongue or her nose. You are NOT getting any piercings while you're with me, OK?'

'OK,' Megan says. Then, as Mum turns to walk away, she mutters, 'But it *is* my money.'

And I'm sure she didn't *mean* Mum to hear. But Mum stops in her tracks and I brace myself. My mother might look all flowery and floaty and soft, but she's like one of those dangerous prehistoric creatures. Not to be messed with. Sure enough, she turns on her heel.

'OK, Megan,' Mum says. 'There's one simple way to sort this out.' And with that she strides over to the man at the body-piercings stall.

'No, Mum, please!' I call. But it's too late. Mum's in full flight.

'That girl,' Mum says loudly, pointing at Megan, 'is only thirteen. She does NOT have permission to have ANY piercings or tattoos.'

And it's like everyone for miles around turns and stares at us.

'Cool,' the man says. 'No worries, lady. We've got a strict policy.' He points to a sign behind him. 'Over sixteens only!' he shouts across to us. 'Got that, girls?'

I roll my eyes – my mum is SO embarrassing sometimes.

Megan stands rooted to the spot, shell-shocked.

And despite the fact that she nearly sent me into full-blown anxiety meltdown yesterday, I do feel sorry for her. There's nothing worse than getting roasted by a mate's mum in full view of the public. I should know. Mrs Ankhar once laid into me in the shopping mall. I was traumatized for months after.

In a show of sisterhood, I link arms with Megan and gently lead her away from the scene of her public humiliation.

'Look on the bright side,' I sigh as Mum disappears off in the opposite direction. 'At least *you* don't have to live with her!'

27

By the time we get back to the yurt I only have ten minutes to get my stuff packed before Zing's due to pick me up. Cordelia, Megan and Taslima get changed into their bikinis to go to the beach. I shove my black skinny jeans and the top Twig gave me into the ruckie for later, along with the cute little camisole top and shorts set Mum got me to replace my fave bra and knickers that Houdini chewed on his first Great Escape. I haven't worn the new set yet, so it'll feel sort of special for tonight.

Just then Zing drives up in an open-top jeep. 'Great news, Sassy!' she says as she leaps down and bounces over. 'Phoenix Macleod wants to do the photo shoot with you!'

'What!' Megan gasps.

'It was Phoenix's idea,' Zing grins. 'Sassy made quite an impression on him.'

Megan lets out a little squeak, like a cat whose tail's just been trod on.

'Of course, he won't be modelling any clothes,'

Zing continues. 'LOVE YOUR PLANET's a girls' range'

'Great,' I smile.

And it *is* great, but I'm a bit worried about being around Phoenix. When I'm near him I feel like I'm cheating on Twig. Even though I know there's no way I would ever let anything happen. I mean, I've given Twig my word, haven't I?

'Ready, then?' Zing asks, checking her watch.

'Yep,' I answer, hoisting my ruckie on to my shoulder.

Zing picks up my guitar and heaves it into the back of the jeep. Mum hugs and kisses me and wishes me luck.

'You'll be fine,' Cordelia grins, coming out into the sunshine to hug me. 'I've got really good vibes about tonight's concert. I've got this hunch, you know, this gut feeling. You're going to blow them away, Sassy Wilde.'

'Yeah,' says Taslima, joining in the hug. 'Just be yourself, Sassy. Sing as if you're in your room, doing it for us.' Then she pushes my hair back and whispers in my ear, 'Just remember to put your clothes on, won't you?'

Pip gives me a big slobbery kiss on each cheek. She's decided she's going to collect autographs and has decorated one of her notebooks as *PIP WILDE'S AUTOGRAPH BOOK*. She thrusts it into my hand.

'Get Phoenix to write something extra special,' she smiles. 'On the very first page.'

'Course I will,' I grin, 'if you promise to be my slave forever.'

'Sassy!' Mum scolds playfully. Then she says to Pip, 'I'm sure Phoenix will write something really sweet. He seems like a lovely boy.'

Which sets Cordelia and Taslima giggling.

'Ready, Sassy?' Zing calls as she starts up the engine.

I give everyone one last big hug – even Megan – then climb up into the jeep. Zing drives off and everyone waves. As we round the corner where the track disappears into the wood, I look back to give one last wave to my friends. But they've already left for the beach, and I can just see them, three small figures in bikinis, disappearing in the opposite direction, laughing and chatting.

Something inside me twangs just then. And I have the most awful feeling of loss.

'Everything all right?' Zing asks as I turn back round in my seat. 'You seem a bit quiet.'

'I'm fine,' I force a bright smile. But I'm lying. A bit of me isn't fine. A bit of me wants to forget all about photo shoots and performing and Phoenix Macleod and trying to be a star.

A bit of me wants to jump out and run back and join my bezzies on the beach.

28

The performers' enclosure sits on top of the cliffs, a group of big luxury caravan trailers, set apart and fenced off from the public part of the festival.

Zing pulls the jeep up outside one of the trailers. It's the kind of thing I've only ever seen in American movies before. Phoenix Macleod is sitting on the deck of the trailer next door in a pair of faded cut-offs, lazily strumming his guitar. He looks up as I arrive and smiles, but keeps playing, his black curls shining in the sun. And despite my best intentions to stay faithful to Twig forever, my heart flips over.

Inside the trailer Chantelle, the make-up lady, is waiting for me, with a specially lit mirror and a huge make-up box like the one we keep tools in at home. She grins a big warm hello. She's not at all what I was expecting. I thought she'd be skinny and glamorous, but she's plump and jovial. Zing shows me a small room at the back of the trailer where I can dump my stuff. She's made a big gold star and stuck it on the door.

'Not the best dressing room ever,' she laughs, 'but better than some I've seen, and you can have a nap here after the photo shoot.'

'It's great,' I say, throwing my ruckie down on the bed and propping my guitar against the wall.

Then I go back through to the living area of the trailer and Chantelle sits me down in front of the mirror.

'Think of me as a fairy godmother,' she says as she stands behind me, looking at my reflection. 'Not that I'm going to be messing about with any old pumpkins!' she laughs. 'No, no, girl. I'm simply going to make you look your very best. And I think we'll start with your hair.'

'I like my hair the way it is,' I say right away.

'Don't worry!' Chantelle laughs, and her curls dance. 'I like your hair too. It's great, got character, but you just let me use a little magic, and we can make it even better.'

And with that she sets to work with a pair of heated tongs. Half an hour later my hair is falling down in the most gorgeous, glossy corkscrew curls you could imagine.

'Do you trust me now, sweetie?' Chantelle smiles, holding a hand mirror up so I can see the back of my head.

I nod.

'So now for a little make-up. And don't even start to protest!' she says when I open my mouth. 'How do you think models in magazines look so good in their photos? None of that's natural, I can tell you. I've worked with the best, and they all, every last one of them, wake up with zits on their noses and shadows under their eyes. That little ole camera can be cruel. So let Chantelle make your skin as perfect as possible, and bring out the sparkle in those beautiful eyes!'

Chantelle's so nice, it's hard to argue with her. She spins my chair round so I'm facing her rather than the mirror, then starts cleansing my face with soft cream on cotton-wool pads. It's warm inside the trailer. And outside Phoenix is strumming his guitar softly and singing. I start to feel sleepy, and give in happily to my fairy godmother as she orders me to close my eyes, relax my face muscles, tip up my chin, open my eyes, smile, pout, purse.

Chantelle's fingers are gentle and the different make-ups and creams smell lovely, like a mix of Mum's perfume and the kind of sweeties I loved when I was tiny.

'Now if you don't like what I've done,' Chantelle says as she flicks a soft smattering of powder over my face and I screw my eyes tight shut, 'then don't you worry your pretty little head. We'll take it all off and start again.'

With that she spins me round to face the mirror.

'Wow!' I gasp. 'Is that me?'

'You like it, sweetie?' Chantelle asks, rearranging some of my new glossy corkscrew curls.

'It's cool,' I gasp. And I mean it. I never guessed in a thousand years I could look like that! It's like I've got no make-up on at all, but my eyes look much bigger, my lashes look naturally thick and curled, my skin is radiant, and my lips look, well, luscious, actually!

Just then there's a tap at the open door of the trailer and Phoenix sticks his head in.

'I think they're wanting us for the photo shoot,' he says. Then he looks at me for what feels like forever and blows softly through his lips.

My heart starts to thunder so loud I'm sure he'll hear it.

'They want you to bring your guitar,' he smiles, then disappears.

'Have a good one, precious,' Chantelle says as she starts to pack her toolbox again, 'and don't let *anyone* mess with your hair!'

'I won't!' I promise. Then I grab my guitar and head out to the jeep, my shiny new corkscrew curls bouncing in the sun.

29

Zing takes us to a small marquee tent near the stalls. It's been specially set up as the wardrobe room for the photo shoot. Some of the festival-goers watch as we climb down from the jeep. A ripple of excitement runs through the crowd when they see Phoenix, and some people take photos. Then Zing bundles us into the tent and introduces us to Anna from *Tween Qween Magazine*.

'She looks absolutely perfect!' Anna gushes as she circles me, looking me up and down like I'm a prize racehorse. Then she ushers me over to a rail of clothes.

'Look, I'll wait outside,' Phoenix says. 'This is your gig, Sassy. Think of me as a prop . . . a piece of scenery.'

'Isn't he gorgeous?' Anna gasps in an exagger-ated whisper before he's even outside the tent.

And I have to admit to myself that, in fact, he is. I finger Twig's friendship bracelet thoughtfully. Somehow touching it makes him feel more real, helps me resist my attraction to Phoenix.

'Oh no, no, NO!' Anna gasps, taking my hand and frowning at the raggedy friendship bracelet. '*That* will have to go!'

I'm about to explain that I can't take it off, even for the photo shoot, because the threads have tightened themselves into an impossible knot, when suddenly, as if from nowhere, Anna produces a tiny pair of scissors and snips it in two!

'Ou-ou-ouw!' I squeal, outraged.

'Omigod!' Zing exclaims. 'You're not cut, are you, Sassy? Is she bleeding?'

I stare down at my naked wrist. Twig's friendship bracelet lies on the floor, its perfect circle broken.

'N . . . no,' I stammer. Anna picks the broken bracelet up. I take it from her silently. Cos I know if I say anything I'll say everything and we can forget all about the photo shoot, and then Y-Gen will probably think I'm unstable and tell me not to bother doing the warm-up for Phoenix tonight, and I'll be letting Cordelia and Taslima and Pip and Mum and Dad – and Twig, and most especially Twig – down. So I keep all my rage bottled as I hold Anna's gaze.

'You had no right to do that,' I say, my voice an angry whisper.

Anna shrugs. 'We'll get you another,' she mutters, taking some money from a cash box on the table behind her. 'Kara!' she shouts and a girl not much older than me comes running over. 'Go to one of the stalls. Get one of those friendship bracelet things.'

'No, don't bother!' I blurt. 'There's no point. It's a friendship bracelet. You can't just replace it with a new one.'

Kara stops in her tracks and looks to Anna. Anna raises her eyebrows at Zing, then claps her hands in a businesslike way. 'Chop-chop, everyone. We have a photo shoot to do here. Let's get moving!'

'You OK, Sassy?' Zing asks quietly as Anna strides off, barking orders. 'Anna can be a bit . . . impetuous . . . at times. But she's really good at what she does.'

'I'm fine,' I say coldly. Right at that moment I just want to get the photo shoot over and done with. I want to get back to the trailer and play guitar for a while. Playing guitar always helps when I feel hurt. My music is like this warm place I can crawl into, like a big soft duvet of sound. Once I'm inside nothing can get at me. Nothing can hurt me. It's just me and the music.

Zing apologizes so much for Anna, I have to tell her to stop.

'It's OK,' I insist. 'It wasn't your fault.' I make a mental note, though, to tell Cordelia what Anna did. And if she wants to take a little revenge by sending some bad karma[22] Anna's way, I won't stop her.

Then I'm swept up in the photo shoot. The clothes are really cool. There's a woman called Zandra in charge of them and each outfit is lined up in the order it's needed for the shoot. The photographer, Arthur, who's really fun, has made up a kind of storyboard that Phoenix and I have to follow.

The first shots are in the woods. I'm wearing a super little vest-top in a funky shade of green, with coordinated long shorts and groovy sandals.

'I don't know how you feel about this,' Arthur says, 'but I'd love a shot of you up a tree. Maybe we could get a ladder from somewhere to help you up?' He turns to Kara. 'Kara! Ladder? Try the roadies, darling!'

And I'm saying, 'No! No!'

'What? You don't want to do the tree, sweetheart?' Arthur asks, crestfallen.

I don't answer. Instead I start climbing and in seconds I've swung myself on to a branch, my legs dangling over, exactly the way Arthur has storyboarded it.

'Wow!' Arthur exclaims, looking at me through the camera. 'Brilliant! You're a star, Sassy Wilde!'

'It's her natural habitat,' Zing smiles.

---

[22] Like a plague of spiders in her undies drawer.

Then Phoenix climbs up beside me and Kara passes us our guitars. Arthur tells us to play a bit together, so I let Phoenix lead and I try to follow his chords. More than once I get it wrong and Phoenix's eyes meet mine and he laughs and I laugh too, and I can't believe how lovely he is.

'Brilliant! Fantastic! Awesome!' Arthur coos as his camera clicks and whirrs.

We do some other shots too. Among the stalls. First I wear a little navy-blue skirt dotted with coloured stars, and a long-sleeved Tee with a dolphin leaping across its front.

Then I'm changed into a gorgeous creamy lace blouse and a flouncy short coffee-coloured skirt, with flat thong sandals that lace up to the knee. Kara puts a string of delicate shell beads round my neck and winds another shell necklace round and round each of my wrists. It feels all feminine. Not at all like me. When I emerge from the tent, Phoenix makes a low bow.

'I feel sort of under-dressed in my jeans, Princess Sassy.'

'Why thank you, Prince Charming!' I say and curtsey. 'I think you look just perfect.'

'So do you,' Phoenix says, holding my gaze. The colour rushes to my cheeks. There's a flash as a bystander takes a photo.

'Told you I was your fairy godmother, didn't I?'

Chantelle chortles as she appears to set my cork-screw curls in place.

Arthur wants us to mess about in front of a stall with all these crazy hats. Anna shoos all the other festival-goers back, so it's just me and Phoenix in the shot.

'Phoenix, I want you to put one of the hats on Sassy,' Arthur shouts. But the first three Phoenix chooses won't go on properly cos of all my curls, then Phoenix jokes it must be my head that's too big and what will it be like if I ever get a hit, and we're both laughing when Arthur shouts, 'Hold it! That's it! That's the one!'

We freeze. Phoenix is placing a mad rainbow-coloured hat on my head, gazing straight into my eyes and I'm gazing into his, and normally I would have looked away, you know, but Arthur's shouting, 'Hold! Hold! Hold!' and the camera's going click click click and time stops, and my heartbeat starts to race, and it's like suddenly I'm underwater. I'm drowning.

'Grrrreat!' Arthur shouts. 'Got it!' At last I tear my eyes away from Phoenix, and with a plunk like a cork being pulled from a bottle, I plop back into the sounds and colours of the real world.

By the time we get back to the performance trailers I'm pretty tired. Ben's there waiting. I yawn and go through to the toilet to freshen up.

I close the door, but in the small space of the trailer I can still hear Ben and Zing chatting.

'How did the photo shoot go?' Ben asks.

'Great!' Zing replies enthusiastically. 'You were absolutely right. Sassy's a natural in front of the cameras. *And* we got a bonus, there's a real chemistry between her and Phoenix –'

I look at myself in the mirror. It's true. There is something between me and Phoenix. I feel it every time I'm near him. And I know he does too. And I don't know what to do about it.

I sit down on the toilet lid and take Twig's broken friendship bracelet from my pocket and run it through my fingers. It's frayed and faded and tatty. But that doesn't make it any less special.

I close my eyes and lean against the wall for a moment. What's wrong with me? How can I feel like this about both Twig and Phoenix? Not that long ago I didn't particularly like any boys. Not that way. Oh yeah, there was Magnus . . . But then I met Twig . . .

For a moment I think of asking Zing if I can use her mobile. Twig seems so far away. It's only a couple of days since I saw him, but already it's really hard to remember what he looks like. If I could talk to him he would feel real again, and I could explain what happened to the friendship bracelet. But there's no point. Twig doesn't have a mobile. I could try his landline, but the chances are he won't be at home. He's much more likely to be out up a tree somewhere . . .

Just then there's a tap at the bathroom door.

'Sassy!' Zing calls softly. 'Are you OK in there?'

'Yeah! Just coming!' I call. 'Everything's fine!'

But I'm not sure it is.

30

'Let's just do a quick check on what you're performing tonight,' Zing says when I at last sit down at the little table on the deck. 'Then you should have a rest.' She checks a pile of papers on her lap. 'Chantelle will do your hair and make-up again at half six. You're on stage at half seven.'

Ben looks at me, concerned. 'You're not your usual smiling self, Sassy,' he says. 'Doing the photo shoot's not tired you out too much, has it?'

'No way,' I answer, forcing thoughts of Twig and Phoenix from my mind. 'It was great. Kept me from getting nervous about tonight.'

'That's my girl!' Ben pours three tall glasses of chilled Hi-Vi. 'Being a music star isn't just about getting up on stage and singing a few songs. It's a pretty gruelling lifestyle at times. You need stamina.' He raises his glass and chinks it with mine. 'And so far, Sassy, you're doing great.'

'OK, star girl,' Zing says brightly. 'Tell us what you're planning to play for your set tonight.'

'I want to start with "Why Must My Dad Try to Ruin My Life",' I say.

'Mmmm . . .' says Ben. 'It's upbeat. Punchy. Should wake them up a bit. Get their attention. I'm cool with that.'

'Then I thought I might do a love song, something slower, like "Pinch Me, I Must Be Dreaming".'

'Sounds good,' Zing says.

'I want to finish with something a bit different.' I pause. I know they're not going to like what I'm going to say next, so I say it quickly. '"Sweatshop Kid".'

Ben and Zing exchange a look.

'Yeah . . . the first two sound great,' Zing says slowly. 'But I'm not on for finishing with "Sweatshop Kid". What do you think, Ben?'

Ben shakes his head. 'It's not you at your best, kiddo. It's a bit too . . .' He waves his hands in the air, as if trying to grasp something invisible.

'Too hard-hitting?' I suggest.

'That's it!' Zing nods her head enthusiastically. 'You're a bright girl. I knew you'd understand. Right now we have to get everyone to love you. We don't want people to think about –'

'About what they're doing to the world!' I exclaim. 'But I do. Don't you see? That's why I sing. What we do in one part of the world affects people and animals and birds and everything all over the world! I WANT people to think about that!'

Zing stands up, clearly annoyed. She walks to the edge of the deck and stands with her back to us, staring out to sea. Ben sighs heavily.

'We understand that, Sassy,' Ben says in a quiet voice. 'Of course we do. And "Sweatshop Kid" is a great song. Very you. Perfect to put on your first album.' He looks me straight in the eye and his smile fades. 'If we decide to sign you, that is.'

I take a sharp breath in. 'Don't try to blackmail me!' I say angrily. 'Cos it won't work.'

'Look,' says Zing firmly, turning round to face us, 'we're not trying to blackmail you. Your business is writing songs and singing them. Ours is making stars. We know what we're doing. If you want to make it, Sassy, you'll have to work with us. In the short term you might need to make a compromise. But once you've made your name you can sing what you like.' She pauses. 'Do you understand?'

I sigh heavily. 'I suppose so,' I say.

'Good,' says Ben. 'How you feel about the world is important to you. And it's important to us too. It makes you special. But if you want to do a song with a strong message to finish, then how about "When the Little Birds Stopped Singing"? The crowd would love that!'

I think about it for a moment. I don't want to

compromise, but I don't want to blow my chances with Y-Gen Music either. And I do like Ben and Zing. It was a great break them seeing my Internet clip. If I mess up with them, who knows, I might never get the chance with anyone else.

'You did "When the Little Birds Stopped Singing" brilliantly in the studio,' Zing says. 'In fact, we were talking about releasing that as your first single.'

My heart skips a beat. My first single!

'OK,' I say. 'I'll finish up with "When the Little Birds Stopped Singing".'

'Yay!' Zing puts up a hand to high-five me. 'Good choice, Sassy. That's a great set.'

'I agree,' Ben smiles, obviously relieved. 'Now, off you go for a rest. We want you to hit that stage tonight on full power.'

'No worries,' I smile. 'Tonight means everything to me. I'm going to blow them away!'

'That's my girl!' Zing gives me a hug. 'We'll make a superstar of you yet, Sassy Wilde!'

And I so hope she's right!

31

I'm more tired after the photo shoot than I want Ben and Zing to know. So I'm really anxious to get into my little room in the trailer, close the door and lie down. But before I do, I wander over to the edge of the cliff and gaze down at the beach below. The golden sand is crowded. Some people are sunbathing, some running around after frisbees, others splashing in the sea, which looks the most gorgeous shade of blue. I scour the tiny figures, hoping to make out Taslima, Megan and Cordelia, but I guess I'm way too far away.

Suddenly I realize I'm not alone. Phoenix is standing at my shoulder.

'It looks good down there, doesn't it?' he says.

I nod. We stand in silence for a moment. We can just hear the excited shouts and laughter of the bathers above the gentle roll of the waves.

'Do you ever find yourself wishing you were . . . you know . . . like everyone else?' I ask.

'All the time,' Phoenix laughs. Then his face

goes serious. 'Well, maybe not all the time. But some of the time, sure. Mostly I just get on with it. I've wanted to sing and perform for as long as I can remember.'

'Me too,' I smile. 'Mum says I used to sing in my pram. When I was two or three I used to sing out in the garden. I would make poor old Brewster sit and listen while I danced around him waving my arms, belting out "You Put a Spell On Me". And once I was singing so loud this grumpy old neighbour shouted out the window and told me to shut up!'

'Yeah, I was a bit like that,' Phoenix smiles. 'But sometimes I wish I wasn't the one up on the stage, that I could be in the audience with my mates, having a laugh.'

'Do you still see them? Your mates, I mean. It kinda worries me that if I get a recording deal I'll lose my friends . . .' my voice trails off. This is the first time I've admitted to anyone that I do have doubts about going down the whole stardom route.

Phoenix's face clouds. 'I can only say what happened with me. It might be different for you. But I'm not one of the crowd any more. Not really. I mean, when I'm back home my mates try to count me in. But I'm always missing out on things. They have mad in-jokes and I don't know what they're on about. It kinda hurts. But you've just got to get on with it, haven't you?'

'I suppose so,' I sigh. 'It's like I want it both ways. I want to be a normal everyday girl, doing things with my best buds . . . And I want to be up on that stage singing. I want to be a star.'

Phoenix is quiet for what feels like a long time. 'People like us,' he says at last, 'I don't know if we totally have the choice. It's like you've been given this one thing you're really good at. It might be football, or acting or even something like maths –'

Immediately I think of Taslima with her calculator brain.

'– and if you don't use it,' Phoenix continues, 'if you don't do something with it, you don't try your best to see how far you can go, then you're letting yourself down. And everyone else. My mates wanted me to go for it. They knew they couldn't do it, but they really wanted me to.'

'Yeah, I guess you're right. Taslima and Cordelia have always been right behind me too. I mean, if I mess up tonight –'

'You're not going to mess up,' Phoenix says. Gently, he takes my hands in his and looks straight into my eyes so my heart melts and slides right down to my feet. 'You're going to be great.'

32

As soon as I lie down on the trailer bed I fall into a deep and dreamless sleep. Zing wakes me with a fruit smoothie and a plate of sandwiches.

'It's just after six,' she says quietly. 'Chantelle's here. So have a shower, come through when you're ready and she'll sort your hair and make-up. Oh, and can you give me what you're wearing tonight and I'll get it ironed? There's a robe for you in the shower room. And a shower cap. Chantelle says not to wash your hair, she'll just tidy the curls up a bit.'

'I don't think my stuff needs ironing,' I say sleepily as I dig my clothes out of my ruckie. But I'm so wrong! Twig's T-shirt is totally crumpled.

'Just as well I asked!' Zing smiles as she takes the stuff from me. 'See you in five, then!'

I pile my hair into the shower cap and stumble into the shower. As the hot water streams over me I run back over the conversation with Phoenix. He's right. If you've got a talent you've got to use

191

it. Otherwise you'd spend your whole life wondering if you could have made it. If you could have made a difference.

I dry myself off with a big fluffy towel – fit for a star – and put on the new camisole and shorts undies I've been keeping especially for tonight. Then I wrap myself up in the cosy white robe and hurry through to let Chantelle work her magic on my face.

'So,' says Chantelle as she strokes some cleanser on to my skin, 'I see you found your Prince Charming this afternoon.'

'He's not my Prince Charming!' I object, my colour rising. 'Anyway, I'm not looking for a boyfriend.'

Chantelle smoothes the faintest hint of foundation on my face with a soft brush. 'But Phoenix is such a dish! Why, if I was twenty years younger . . .' she laughs, her dark eyes twinkling.

'Yeah, but I've already got a boyfriend. He just couldn't come this weekend.' I finger the friendship bracelet in my pocket. 'So, you see, it doesn't actually matter how sweet Phoenix is.'

Chantelle loads some blusher on to a feathery brush and flicks a tickly lick of it across my cheekbones. 'Well, precious, I admire your loyalty. He must be very special to keep you back from that sugar-pie, Phoenix.'

'He is,' I say quietly.

In no time at all Chantelle finishes my make-up, then she quickly tongs my corkscrew curls, so I look all fresh and shiny again. I check my watch. It's almost seven. I had expected Zing back ages ago. While Chantelle packs the make-up back into her toolbox, I pace the trailer. The nerves are beginning to build now.

'Are you OK, sweetie?' Chantelle asks as she's about to leave. 'I really need to go over to Phoenix's trailer now. Give him a final polish.'

'Does he wear make-up?' I gasp, astonished.

'Not so much *make-up*.' Chantelle waves an imaginary wand. 'More like a little *magic*!'

Just then Zing comes running up, all hot and bothered, and Chantelle leaves on her next fairy godmother mission.

'I am SO, SO sorry, Sassy,' Zing says breathlessly. 'I meant to be back ages ago. There was a problem, but I've solved it. Anyway, how are you feeling?'

'A bit nervous,' I admit, pacing up and down. 'But that's OK. I think I'd be more worried if I didn't feel nervous. I mean, I usually feel nervous before I'm doing something that makes me nervous, then when I'm doing it I stop being nervous and I'm . . .' I take a breath. '. . . fine.' I gulp another breath. 'Sorry! When I'm nervous I kinda rabbit on a bit, but you were saying there was a problem?'

Zing takes something from the bag she's holding.

'This,' she says quietly.

It's my T-shirt. But not my T-shirt. Because where Twig had painted the beautiful blue Planet Earth, there's now a huge hole, all singed brown round the edges.

'I'm so sorry, Sassy. The iron wasn't even that hot.' Zing shoves her hand through the hole. 'All the colours came off and stuck to it.'

I stare at the rag Zing's holding. 'But I can't wear it now!' I gasp. My mouth goes dry as the panic starts to bubble up inside me.

'Course not!' Zing says, suddenly brightening. 'Didn't I say there was a problem – but I solved it?'

She pulls something from another bag. It's the pretty cream lace blouse and the little flounced skirt I liked so much on the photo shoot this afternoon. The outfit Phoenix said I looked so good in. 'Isn't it great?' Zing spreads the outfit on the sofa. 'Anna saved the day. Look, she's even given me the shell necklaces. She says you can keep them too. So what do you think?'

I take a deep breath and sink down on to a chair. Twig made me a special top to wear for my first big gig and now it's a sorry rag with a big hole burned right through it.

'But this was a special Tee,' I stammer, picking

up the singed remains. 'I really wanted to wear it tonight.' I hear my own voice. Childish, like Pip. Tears spring up at the back of my eyes and I fight them back.

'I'm SO sorry, honey,' Zing sighs. 'But look on the bright side. You looked absolutely fab in this stuff.'

I stare dejectedly at the pretty blouse. Zing checks her watch. 'Look, I don't want to rush you, but we really don't have time to mess around, Sassy. We should be backstage by now.'

'OK,' I sigh, picking up the fashion-shoot outfit. 'I'll just be a minute.'

I'm in my room changing when something occurs to me. Is it possible that Zing and Ben keep creating situations for me to see how I cope? They spring a photo shoot on me with hardly any notice. They ruin the one thing I really wanted to wear for my first performance. Maybe, just maybe, I think as I pull the blouse on and step into the skirt and zip it up, they're testing me. Trying to see how adaptable I can be under stress.

In which case, I think, as I pick my guitar up and check my reflection in the mirror, they're going to find out that Sassy Wilde is not easily fazed.

This girl can deal with anything they throw at her!

33

Backstage is chaos when we arrive. Things have to be organized not just for Phoenix, but for his backing band too, and for the bands that will be on later. Roadies and techies are milling about, trailing black flexes, setting mike stands in place, flashing the spots off and on.

Zing takes me to a tiny quiet space just behind the big main power supply, where Ben's standing watching the final preparations.

'Now, whatever you do, Sassy,' Ben teases as we pass, 'don't touch that switch.' He points to the huge red mains handle. 'We know what you're like about saving power.'

I roll my eyes and force a laugh. I know Ben's only trying to lighten things up a bit.

'This is the closest you'll get to a dressing room on this kind of gig,' Zing says as she dumps her bag on one of the chairs and goes off to find the guy who'll be on the soundboards. 'Got to double-check everything!' she says. 'You can tune up here, Sassy.'

I take my guitar out of its case and strap it on. It always feels good when I put my guitar on. If I had to perform without it I'd feel quite naked. When it's in front of me it's like it protects me. In a few minutes I've finished tuning up, but my legs feel a bit wobbly, so I sit down on the edge of one of the chairs. I check my watch. The minutes tick slowly. I feel very, very lonely.

Then suddenly, who should appear from nowhere but Pip! In the prettiest dress imaginable. She twirls a few times, then bows deeply.

'Surprise!' she grins. 'Mum got it for me at one of the stalls. AND it's fair trade, so Mum says everyone who made it got paid properly.'

Then Cordelia and Taslima and Megan appear, grinning and giggling.

'Surprise!' Cordelia says, her green eyes flashing.

'We just had to see you –' Taslima laughs.

'To wish you luck!' Megan finishes.

Suddenly my nerves disappear and a big grin bursts out on my face. I take my guitar off and perch it against a chair, then we all have a great big hug.

'It's so good to see you guys!' I exclaim. 'I thought you'd forgotten all about me!'

'Don't be so silly!' Taslima smiles gently. 'We've been missing you.'

'Yeah,' says Megan. 'We keep saying, *Oh, Sassy*

would have loved this, or *we know exactly what Sassy would say about that*.'

'Really?' I ask, and I guess they hear the worry in my voice.

'You're our bezzie, Sass,' Cordelia gives me a hug. 'We'd never forget about you!'

'We made this for you.' Megan hands me a card.

'Yeah, I can guess who designed this!' I laugh. On the front is a spiky black cat with bright green eyes. At the top it says *GOOD LUCK, SASSY!*

'Well, you might be wrong,' Taslima smiles quietly. 'Cos I did.'

'And Megan and me coloured it in!' Pip pipes up.

I wanted to give you this too,' Megan hands me a pale-blue stone. It's the angelite egg from the 'healing crystals' stall. 'I thought it might help.'

'Thanks, Megan,' I say, and for the first time since our big fall-out in P7 I feel kinda close to her, like she really could be a best bud again.

Out front someone is saying *one two one two* over the sound system.

'I think I'm going to have to run to the loo!' I gasp, so we all have one last quick hug.

'You'll blow them away, Sass,' Cordelia says as she turns to leave. 'I know you will. I've got this gut feeling about it.'

'Yeah, so have I!' I laugh as I leg it to the nearest toilet.

When I get back my best buds have gone and Zing's waiting for me.

'I like your flowers,' she says as I check myself in the dusty old mirror that's been propped backstage for the performers. 'They're gorgeous. And so right for you. Wild flowers for Sassy Wilde.'

'Flowers?' I repeat. 'What flowers?'

'Those flowers?' Zing points to a pretty bunch of wild meadow flowers, all pinks and blues and golds and purples, sitting beside my guitar. 'They'll be from Phoenix,' she adds. 'That's SO the kind of thing he would do.'

Just then Zing's phone rings. She answers quickly, says a few words, then flicks it off again.

'Well!' she says. 'The TV cameras are here to get some footage of Phoenix. That boy is super-hot at the moment. And as they're all set up, who knows, they might well take some of you too.'

'What? TV cameras? Will I be on the telly?' I gasp. My tummy's so full of butterflies I swear it could be declared a site of scientific interest.

'Don't get too excited!' Zing says as she goes to stuff the mobile into her already overfull bag. 'They film hours of stuff, then they show about three seconds on TV. Best not get your hopes up, but you never know!'

Just then Zing's bag tips over and her papers go flying all over the floor.

'Leave them!' Zing says sharply as I immediately bend to gather them up.

But her words come too late.

A letter has landed at my feet. From *Tween Qween Magazine*. And my name's on it. Zing goes to snatch it away but I stamp my foot on it. Across the top it says:

PHOTO SHOOT – PARADISO'S NEW TEEN RANGE – LOVE YOUR PLANET.

'Paradiso's!' I gasp. As I pick the letter up the awful truth slowly begins to dawn on me. 'You never told me I was modelling for Paradiso's!'

Zing shrugs, tugs the letter from my hand and stuffs it into her bag. 'Would you have done it if I had?'

'Of course not! Their clothes are made in Third World sweatshops! They use child labour and pay them slave wages. That's why they're so cheap!'

'Yeah, but they are a hundred per cent organic and environmentally friendly,' Zing mutters as she scoops up the rest of the fallen papers and slides them back into her bag. 'Look, Sassy,' she sighs, 'the world's not perfect. Like we said before, it's best to leave the business side to us. You DO want to be a star, don't you?'

'Yeah, but not at any price!' I place my guitar back into its case and bang the lid shut.

'What are you doing?' Zing says, alarmed.

'I'm going home!'

'You can't!' She stands in front of me. 'There's hundreds of people out there. All expecting a concert. And you have an agreement with Y-Gen Music.'

'Stuff Y-Gen Music!' I mutter, angrily snapping shut the clips on my guitar case. 'You're not the only recording company in the world.'

'Sassy.' Zing puts a hand on my arm and I shrug it off. 'If you don't go out there and play tonight no other recording company will touch you. Ever. There's kids queuing up, all wanting their chance, their big break. If you pull out and let the audience down, no one else will ever take you on. Not Y-Gen. Not anyone. Do you understand?'

I take a deep breath in.

Time stands still for a long moment.

Zing's right. And I know it.

She checks her watch. 'The decision's yours,' she says, picking up her bag. 'You're due on stage in five minutes.'

And with that she leaves.

34

I pace the small space, thoughts swirling in my head like leaves. Can I really just walk away from this, my one chance at breaking through? How many nights have I dreamed of getting to this point?

I pick up the bunch of flowers and bury my face in them, as if their scent might calm me. A tiny envelope falls to the floor. I pick it up and open it with shaky fingers. The card's handmade, not much bigger than a matchbox, with a crazy curly-haired girl hand-drawn on the front. Playing guitar. A big silver star shining above her.

I open it up. Inside it says one word.

TWIG.

TWIG! My pulse quickens. I spin round, almost expecting to see him there.

But I'm alone. There's no one else. What a fool I am! Of course Twig's not here. He probably made the card before we left and gave it to Megan to give to me.

The voice of the MC booming through the

loudspeakers startles me back to reality. He's warming the crowd up, telling them what a great night they're going to have. Every so often the crowd cheers.

I sink on to a chair and try to collect my thoughts. If only Taslima was here, she'd probably give me good advice. Or if Cordelia was around I'd ask her to cast a magic spell and put time back to before that stupid photo shoot.

Just then Phoenix sticks his head round the curtain. 'Have a good one, Sassy,' he grins, giving me a thumbs up. 'WOW! You look *great* in that outfit!'

Then he's gone. And I'm alone. And that's when I realize just how cleverly Zing has stitched me up. I've modelled Paradiso's latest range of clothes for them. Paradiso's! I probably won't be able to stop those photos going into *Tween Qween Magazine* now. And no one will ever know I was conned into doing it.

I am SO angry! But if I let my anger whoosh up what good will that do? I take Twig's friendship bracelet from my pocket and run it through my fingers like worry beads.

Suddenly my mind's made up. Zing's right on this much. This is my big chance and I'm a fool if I don't use it.

Out on the other side of the stage the crowd cheers again.

Hurriedly, my fingers fumbling, I undo the clips of my guitar case. I tie the broken friendship bracelet round its neck, just under the tuning pegs, then strap the guitar on.

The MC is announcing my name, and the crowd is cheering, and I think of Taslima and Cordelia and Megan and Mum and Pip all down at the front, waiting for me to do what I came here to do.

To sing. To be the one and only Sassy Wilde.

My heart thudding against my ribs, I take a deep breath and burst out on to the stage.

35

The crowd's huge. A sea of colour filling the whole field.

The applause dies down as I approach the front of the stage.

'Hi!' I say into the mike. 'I'm Sassy Wilde. And I'd like to sing for you.'

A small cheer goes up. As I pick out the first few chords I notice Zing in the wings at the side of the stage. She gives me a triumphant smile and a thumbs up, but I don't smile back.

Then I'm singing. And everything else fades away. Because that's what it's like when I sing.

At the end of the first number the crowd applauds. I spot Cordelia and Taslima and Megan right down at the front, waving a big banner saying *SASSY, YOU'RE A STAR!* Beside them Mum and Pip are clapping their hands above their heads and whooping and hollering.

'That's my mum down there,' I say to the crowd. 'She's a bit over-enthusiastic.'

Everyone laughs and somebody shouts, 'Go, Sassy, go!' Out of the corner of my eye I see Phoenix standing at the side of the stage.

'This second number's a kind of love song,' I say into the mike and my voice booms out over the huge speakers. 'I'm only thirteen –' a huge cheer goes up from the crowd and I wait for it to die down – 'but I'm old enough to know when I've met someone special. This next song's for him.'

I try not to look towards the side of the stage, but even so, I know Phoenix is there, watching. I strum the guitar gently and start 'Pinch Me, I Must Be Dreaming'. It's a slow song, moody and romantic, and the crowd seems to hold its breath while I sing.

Pinch me, I think I must be dreaming,
The sky is so blue, my head's light as a cloud
And you're by my side, like I'm dreaming out loud
It's too good to be true, that I'm walking with you
Cos you are the boy makes my heart fill with joy
Oh pinch me, I think I must be dreaming . . .

I pick up the pace as the song goes on, building it faster and louder, then I finish with a deep bow.

The crowd explodes with applause. I glance towards the side of the stage. Zing punches the air. Phoenix is gazing at me, a half-smile on his face. Once again I wait for the applause to die down. I've spotted the TV cameras now, but I try to ignore them, to follow Taslima's advice, to simply be myself. I take a deep breath.

'Before I sing this last song,' I begin, taking the mike from its stand, 'I'd like to ask Pip – that's my little sister – to come up here with me.' There's a squeal of excitement from Pip, then the crowd moves apart to let her through. A tall guy at the front hoists her up on to the stage and she dances across to me, her face shining, and gives me a big hug.

'Pip's the best little sis in the world,' I continue, 'and last week she got a new dress from Paradiso's. But she took that dress back to the store. And I'd like her to tell you why.'

I push the mike under Pip's nose.

'Because Paradiso's clothes are made in sweat-shops by little kids,' Pip says in a tiny voice into the mike. The crowd goes *Aaaahh*, and *Awwww*, and someone shouts *Shame on them*.

'Thanks, Pip,' I say, taking the mike back, then I take a deep breath and address the audience again. 'And the thing is, I've just discovered that the clothes I was given to wear tonight were made by Paradiso's too,' I say, clipping the mike on to its stand. 'By kids as young as Pip, working long hours. So before I sing my last song there's something I want – no, there's something I NEED – to do. And I'm doing it for all the sweatshop kids in the world!'

I take my guitar off and pass it to Pip to hold. Then I unbutton the lacy cream blouse and pull it off and throw it to the floor. The crowd gasps. I step out of the little flouncy skirt and kick it towards Zing. She fires me an angry look, and I guess I've just blown my chances of ever getting a recording contract. Pip's mouth hangs wide open. Coolly, I take my guitar back from her and strap it over my pretty camisole and shorts – which, let's face it, are more modest than anything Arizona Kelly has EVER worn on stage.

Then I strum my guitar REALLY LOUD a few times and launch into 'Sweatshop Kid', belting it out, high energy. In no time the crowd's roaring and clapping along.

When I reach the second chorus I hold the mike down so Pip can sing too. Then everyone joins in. It's brilliant. And I'm just getting into the third verse, really bellowing it out, and the whole place is rocking –

When suddenly, the stage lights go off . . .

I'm still singing but my voice is so tiny even I can hardly hear it. I'm strumming my guitar but there's almost no sound. The crowd's singing falters and dies.

Confused, I look round. Zing gives me a little

wave from the side of the stage and a triumphant smile. Of course! She's thrown the mains switch! Turned the electricity off. I stand there, not sure what to do. Some people are shouting and booing now. Zing comes towards me like she's going to try to force me off. When suddenly, in the middle of all the mayhem, this boy weaves through the crowd, and with one leap vaults on to the stage.

It's Twig!

'Hi!' he says as he runs past. And my heart does a spectacular triple back-flip somersault and lands unsteadily in my throat.

Next thing Twig's pulled the big red handle on the mains switch. The lights surge back on. The mike shrieks into life. I strum my guitar and it thunders out over the big speakers. The crowd cheers. Twig plants himself firmly in front of the power switch, daring Zing to try to get past him . . .

And I start singing again.

Even once I've finished and said *thank you, thank you, thank you*, the crowd goes on cheering. Pip curtseys a few times, then dances to the front of the stage where Mum's waiting to lift her down.

Waving and mouthing *thank you*, I head off stage backwards, so my guitar can preserve what bit of dignity I've got left.

'You were awesome,' Twig grins as I reverse past him into the privacy of the wings.

'So were you,' I grin back.

Phoenix is waiting to go on, and I'm wondering what's going to happen.

'Great stuff,' he smiles, then nods at Twig. 'Well done, mate.'

Already the MC is announcing his name. 'Will you please welcome, the one and only Phoenix Macleod!'

'Oh, before I go on, I thought you might like this,' Phoenix says, draping one of his shirts round my shoulders. 'It's OK. They're specially made for me. In Inverness. By my mum.'

For a moment I hold Phoenix's gaze. The crowd's shouting, *Phoe-nix! Phoe-nix! Phoe-nix!*

'Have a good one!' I smile. 'I think you'll find the crowd's warmed up.'

'You bet they are,' he laughs. 'You're a hard act to follow, Sassy Wilde.'

36

Twig packs my guitar into its case while I quickly button up Phoenix's shirt. It's long and looks like a short dress.

'Let's get out of here,' I say, grabbing Twig's flowers. I pick up the little card he made and for a moment our eyes meet.

'Thanks,' I say. 'For everything.'

'Any time,' Twig shrugs.

I smile sadly at the drawing of the guitar-playing girl with the gold star sparkling above her.

'I guess I'm not going to be a star now, am I?'

'Does that worry you?'

I shake my head and my corkscrew curls bounce. 'Nah,' I lie bravely, even though the truth is that it hurts. 'I did tell you I wouldn't sell out . . . You didn't believe me, did you?'

'Sassy,' Twig says. I hold his gaze. His eyes are brown, like dark honey. Warm. His face is inches from mine. And I think, this is it! At last! What I wished for on the first star! Twig is going to kiss me!!

'You *are* a star,' he whispers, his face so close to mine I feel his breath against my cheek . . . when suddenly a huge roadie sticks his hairy face round the curtain.

'Looking for Ben of Y-Gen,' he shouts. 'Have you seen him?'

I shake my head and he disappears, and when I turn back to Twig the moment has passed.

'Let's get out of here,' I say. 'I really don't want to see Ben and Zing. Not tonight.'

Twig grabs my guitar and I lead him out the back way. Together we hurry down the makeshift stairs. As Phoenix finishes his first song a huge round of applause goes up from the crowd. Something twangs in my chest. I loved being out there. I loved singing in front of a huge crowd. I loved hearing their applause. It made me feel totally alive. It's what I've always dreamed of doing. For as long as I can remember.

And now I've blown it.

37

As we push through the festival-goers watching Phoenix, people nudge each other and point towards me. A girl grabs my arm and shouts into my ear, 'Where can I get your CD?' My heart thumps into my stomach. I shake my head. 'You can't,' I say, trying to control the quiver in my voice. 'I don't have a deal.'

'You will have!' she grins. 'You were brilliant.'

Then Mum spots us and waves, and Megan and Cordelia and Taslima and Pip come rushing over and I'm caught up in a round of excited hugs and squealing.

'You were amazing, Sassy!' Megan grins. 'I always knew you could do it! I've always believed in you!'

As she hugs me Taslima whispers in my ear. 'You did the right thing, Sassy. You do know that?'

'Course I do,' I answer, as tears of disappointment well up behind my eyes.

Just then Phoenix plays the opening chords for Megan's fave song – the one she kept playing over and over in the camper on the way here – and I'm glad it's too noisy for anyone to ask me more questions. Megan whoops and sways her hands above her head, and even Taslima and Cordelia are singing along. When he finishes the number the crowd goes crazy.

'I'd like to sing this next song for someone very special . . .' Phoenix announces from the stage when the applause at last dies down. And despite myself, despite the fact that I'm standing right beside Twig and that's where I want to be, my heart skips a beat.

'I only met her recently,' Phoenix continues, 'so I didn't write this song for her. But tonight I want to dedicate it to her –' He strums his guitar and the crowd cheers and a shiver shimmies down my spine, and I daren't allow myself to think what my brain is going ahead and thinking anyway.

'Cos what she did here tonight was really special,' Phoenix says, and the crowd cheers again. 'She spoke up for all the kids in the world who can't make their own voices heard. So, Sassy Wilde, if you're out there, this song is for you!'

He strums the guitar hard a few times, then launches into a fun funky number all about falling in love with a crazy girl. I'm not sure what to think. My head swirls in a kaleidoscope of emotions. I'm gutted that I've blown my record deal. I'm oh-so-happy that Twig is here. And now Phoenix Macleod is singing a song for me!

Then suddenly, I don't just see Phoenix. I see all the crowd. All listening to him, swaying along, singing along. Megan, Cordelia, Taslima, Pip, even Mum. And everything becomes crystal clear. Phoenix is a performer. He's putting on a performance. He's singing for everyone.

But Twig is the real thing. I squeeze his hand and pull him closer. 'I'm glad you're here,' I shout into his ear.

'So am I,' he smiles, his eyes shining. 'Phoenix is really cool, isn't he?'

'Yeah . . . he's cool . . . but not as cool as you.'

Twig turns and looks at me in the moonlight. 'Sorry,' he shouts. 'What did you say?'

I take a deep breath and cup a hand round Twig's ear.

'I SAID, YEAH, PHOENIX IS COOL. BUT NOT AS COOL AS YOU!'

'Heard you first time,' Twig grins. 'Just wanted to hear it again!'

38

When Phoenix finishes his set Mum insists we all head for the yurt. As we pick our way along the woodland path in the bright moonlight Twig tells me about how he arrived at the festival, just before seven.

'But I didn't even know you were coming!' I exclaim. 'Why didn't you tell me?'

Twig shrugs and his tousle of hair falls over his eyes. 'I wasn't going to come. It was a kinda spur of the moment thing. Dad gave me a lift to the station, then I walked the last few miles.'

'Wasn't he worried about you?' Taslima asks.

'I told him Sassy's mum was picking me up. That I'd be sleeping in the camper.'

'Mmmmm . . .' Cordelia narrows her eyes. 'You're not psychic, are you?'

'Not that I know of,' Twig laughs. 'Just pre-pared to take a risk. For something important enough, that is.' He throws me a look I'm happy to catch, and despite my disappointment about the record deal a big rush of happiness froths up inside me.

'I'm glad you came,' I say quietly. 'Like, for a whole lot of reasons.'

'So am I,' Twig smiles. 'I wouldn't have missed your performance for anything.'

Back at the yurt Mum suggests we light a camp-fire while she makes hot chocolate 'to calm us all down a bit'.

'So are you OK, honey?' Mum asks when at last we've all got our cocoa and are settled down round the fire, the orange and red flames crack-ling. 'You know, about . . . well . . . the way things have gone.'

'If I could turn the clock back I wouldn't do any-thing different.' I sigh. 'I don't want to compromise, not about things that really matter to me. I wouldn't be able to live with myself.' Tears prick the back of my eyes again and I bite my bottom lip to stop them spilling over.

Mum hugs me. 'You paid a big price to do the right thing, sweetheart. You made me very proud tonight.'

'You made us all proud,' Taslima says quietly.

'NOT,' Mum says quickly, 'that I approve of you taking your clothes off in public!'

Everyone laughs and I wipe away a few tears that have escaped and are rolling down my cheeks.

'Like you are the LAST person I would EVER have expected to take your clothes off on stage!' Megan giggles.

'I know, it's one of the things I swore I'd never do!' I force a shaky smile. 'At first, when I realized Zing had tricked me into wearing Paradiso's clothes, I wasn't going to go out on stage at all. I even packed my guitar away. Then I thought, if I don't go out and sing, I'll miss the chance to make a point about kids working in sweatshops. So I had this brainwave. Everyone's been down on the beach all day in bikinis. So why should it be such a big deal, really?'

I fall silent as a jeep bounces along the track, its headlamps spotlighting us. Twig moves closer to me and takes my hand. It pulls up outside our yurt, the lights fade and two people jump down. Ben and Zing.

'Hi, Sassy,' Ben calls. 'You left your rucksack.' He swings it out of the back of the jeep.

'Thanks,' I mumble.

As he strides over Zing hangs back in the shadow of the trees.

'I was wondering if we could have a word?' He nods towards the yurt. 'In private.'

'Sure.' Reluctantly, I let go of Twig's hand and get to my feet.

'Maybe I should come with you?' Mum says. I shake my head. I got into this on my own. I know

I did the right thing, but sometimes in this stupid world that still means you have to face the music, you have to put up with people telling you how much you've let them down.

Inside the yurt it's beautiful at night. The golden lanterns glow softly, casting ghostly shadows across the creamy canvas sides. I sit down on a sofa opposite Zing and Ben, feeling, despite the lovely surroundings, that I'm about to face a firing squad.

'So how do you think it went, Sassy?' Ben asks. I look up quickly. That wasn't what I was expecting.

'Actually,' I say, suddenly angry, '*I* thought it went really well!'

Ben nods his head. 'Well, *actually*, so did we,' he says.

'Pardon?' I gasp.

'We thought it went well,' Ben repeats. 'True, it wasn't what we were expecting. And it will be hell trying to sort it out with Paradiso's and *Tween Qween Magazine*. But you played a stormer, kiddo.' A great big grin spreads across his face. 'Your instincts for publicity are amazing. We need to get your first single out there while you're hot.'

'What? My first single? You still want to sign me? I haven't ruined everything?'

'Well, you almost did,' Ben chuckles. 'But the crowd loved you. And so did the press. Our phones have been red hot since you got off stage.

Everyone wants to know who you are, where we found you. We're expecting coverage in most of the papers tomorrow.'

'And the TV crew got it all on film,' Zing adds. 'You're causing a sensation, Sassy. And that's what this business is all about. So no hard feelings, eh?' Zing holds her hand out, but I don't move to take it.

'You lied to me, Zing,' I say quietly.

'I didn't actually lie, Sassy,' she says lightly. 'I just didn't tell you the whole truth. I honestly didn't think it was such a huge deal –'

'Well, it was,'

'I can see that now, and I'm sorry. So no hard feelings, eh?' Her hand is still outstretched, but I don't move.

'OK, Zing. Maybe I can forgive you for setting up the photo shoot, maybe you did think you were just doing your job, but that little accident with the iron and my T-shirt – that was a horrible thing to do.'

'But that *was* an accident!' Zing exclaims. 'Cross my heart, Sassy. I was trying to iron it properly and it just shrivelled up and burned. There was nothing I could do!'

'Really?' I say, searching her face. Truth is, I want to believe her.

'Really,' she says, her face pale. 'I would never have ruined your top on purpose.'

'Listen, Sassy,' Ben interrupts, getting to his feet. 'It's late now. I think we could all do with a good night's sleep. How about we get in touch next week, talk then about you signing with us?'

'Sure,' I say to Ben. 'But if I do sign with you, you've both got to be totally honest with me from here on in. You've got to take the things I believe in seriously.'

'You got it, kiddo,' Ben grins.

And I suppose I have!

I've got a record deal after all!

Whoopee! Whoopee! Whoopee!

39

While I was with Ben and Zing, Cordelia psychically detected another bag of marshmallows in a
corner of the camper van. Mum's just about to
take them from her cos she says everyone's had
too much junk food already when I come leaping
out of the yurt so excited I can hardly tell them
that it's all OK. That I'm getting my chance to
bring out my first single after all!

'Yay!' Cordelia squeals, ripping the bag of
marshmallows open while Mum's ancient brain is
still trying to catch up with what's happening.
'Let's have a celebration!'

'Oh, all right, then,' Mum relents. 'You can
have another fifteen minutes. Twig, I'll make up a
bed for you in the camper. You'll be sleeping with
Brewster tonight.'

'Sounds great,' Twig grins as he sticks a marshmallow on the end of . . . errr . . . a twig – then
holds it in the fire until it flames. When he pulls it
out, it looks gorgeous, all sugary brown in the

firelight. He passes it to me and I pop it in my mouth. It melts with gooey sweetness.

Pip snuggles up to me while Twig roasts another marshmallow for her. 'You were brilliant tonight,' I whisper in her ear.

'I thought so too!' she grins. 'In fact, I thought I was the *real* star. I liked talking into the mike in front of hundreds of people. Maybe I'll go into politics like Dad!'

'Oh no,' Mum groans. 'One in the family's more than enough!'

We all laugh.

'You know what!' Megan says, jumping up excitedly. 'This is our last night here. Why don't I take a photo of us all round the campfire? I'll just get my camera. Back in a minute!' And she runs off into the yurt.

'Talking of cameras,' I say as I sip my hot chocolate, 'there's one thing still bugs me. I never did find out who filmed the video of me singing at the Bluebell Wood and put it up on the Internet.'

'Oh, I know the answer to that,' Twig says quietly as he passes a melted marshmallow to Taslima. 'But I promised I would never tell.'

'Well, I'd really like to know!' I say, grabbing his hand and playfully twisting it so he falls back on the cushions. 'So do I have to force it out of you?'

'You can't make Twig break his promise!'

Cordelia exclaims. 'That wouldn't be fair! He'd get bad luck, like, forever.'

'And I thought you were non-violent!' Twig protests, trying to tug his hand free.

'But I really want to know!' I sigh, releasing Twig from my grip.

'Why?' Taslima asks, watching me from across the dancing flames. 'Why do you want to know?'

I think about it for a few minutes. Why *do* I want to know?

'I guess I'm curious,' I say slowly. 'But I think it's more than that. I guess I want to say thanks. That video's what gave me my big break.'

'Yeah, whoever did it must like you a lot,' says Taslima.

'I think they must be a pretty good friend,' says Cordelia.

And then it clicks. 'You all know, don't you! You all know and you've kept it from me!'

'Well, obviously, *I* know,' Cordelia smiles secretively, her green eyes sparkling in the firelight. 'I am psychic, after all!'

'And *I* know, because I understand human nature and can reason things out,' Taslima teases.

'And I know, cos the person concerned told me,' Twig adds.

'And I DON'T know,' Pip complains drowsily, 'cos no one ever tells me anything!'

'So who was it?' I squeal, frustrated.

'Guess!' says Taslima.

'I'll give you a clue,' says Cordelia. 'The person who did it's right here.'

I look round the faces of my friends, glowing in the dancing light of the fire. Cordelia, licking at a melted marshmallow. Taslima smiling secretively. Twig watching me closely through his fall of hair. Pip, half-asleep in the heat of the flames.

'Maybe not *right* here,' Taslima corrects Cordelia. 'But not very far away.'

'Mum?' I exclaim, and everyone laughs, shaking their heads.

Just then Megan comes out of the yurt, holding up her camera. 'Found it at last!' Cordelia and Taslima exchange a look.

And that's when the penny drops. 'It was you!' I gasp.

Megan looks at me quizzically. 'Me what?'

'You made the video and put it online!' I exclaim.

Even in the darkness I can see Megan's colour rise. 'I thought that was a secret!' she says angrily to Twig.

'I didn't say anything,' Twig shrugs. 'Anyway I think Sassy should know. It was a really cool thing to do.'

'But why didn't you tell me?' I ask.

'Look.' Megan hangs her head as if suddenly

embarrassed. 'Remember like . . . you know . . . that *thing* I did in P7?'

'But that was yonks ago. You were having a tough time at home. We settled all that,' I say, even though I know I'm not being totally honest.

'Well, I still felt like I hadn't done enough,' says Megan. 'Like my conscience wasn't quite clear or something?'

I stare into the flames. Truth is, deep down that's what I'd felt, but I guess I hadn't wanted to admit it, even to myself.

'Anyway,' Megan continues, 'I brought Twig's dad's camcorder, you know the little one that fits in your hand, back to the Bluebell Wood that time, just in case something interesting happened. And later, when I watched the recording, I thought the bit with you singing was awesome, so I put it online.'

'But something I still don't understand,' I say, confused. 'Why didn't you want me to know?'

'Look, I really wanted to be your friend again – but I didn't want you to think I was trying to, you know, *buy* your friendship, like by doing things for you.' She sighs deeply. 'I just wanted you to like me for being me.'

I look at Megan with fresh eyes. It takes guts to say that kind of thing in front of everyone. And I know, at last, that I can trust her. That we can be friends again.

'But I do like you. And you are my friend.' I wrap my arms round her and give her a great big hug.

'Really?' Megan asks, her voice wobbly with uncertainty.

'OK, sometimes things you do bug me,' I joke. 'But I guess I can be pretty annoying too!'

'I can vouch for that,' Mum mutters as she wanders past. 'In fact, Sassy, I'm just going to pop over to Kris's yurt for a nightcap. I know what you told that poor man. I am NOT on medication!'

Cordelia starts to giggle. As if it's infectious, Megan and me start up too. Twig sticks another marshmallow in the fire, rolls his eyes and says, 'What is it with girls and giggling?'

Taslima opens her mouth like she's going to give him a rational explanation, but Megan looks at her and that's it, she's off. And it feels SO good, to be giggling round a campfire with my three bezzies and my boyfriend, roasting marshmallows!

Life doesn't get any better than this, does it?

Soon Megan, Cordelia, Taslima and me are all snuggled up in our sleeping bags in the yurt. Pip's already disappeared off to the Land of Nod, happily clutching her autograph book. Phoenix wrote a really special message to her in gold ink and she's thrilled to bits. She says she plans to marry him – when she's a bit older, of course.

227

'I've been thinking about something,' I say into the silence.

'What's that?' Cordelia yawns.

'About triangles and friends and things. I was thinking, maybe a triangle's not the best shape for a friendship. But a rectangle's not right either. That just sounds silly.'

Taslima turns over and props herself up on one elbow. 'I've been thinking about that too. Friendships don't come in triangles or rectangles,' she says. 'They come in circles.'

'Of course,' I sigh into the darkness. 'A circle's a good shape. A friendship circle.'

'Then it doesn't matter how many friends are in it,' Taslima explains in her soft voice. 'Three, four or five. All that matters is that it remains unbroken.'

'So am I in the circle now?' Megan says quietly.

'Course you are,' Cordelia says sleepily.

'You have been for ages,' Taslima adds.

'Yeah,' I smile. 'It just took me a while to realize . . .'

The yurt falls quiet.

Strands of music float across on the still night air from the main stage. I wonder if Phoenix is back in his trailer on the cliffs now, sitting out on his deck, all alone, staring across the ink-black sea, quietly strumming his guitar.

Then I think about all my friends – my

friendship circle – surrounding me. I always want to be in the circle. And I want to be a star too. I guess I'm just going to have to work extra hard so I can do both . . .

I yawn and turn over and pull my sleeping bag up around my ears. Slowly, happily, I drift into sleep.

40

Back home at last!

To chaos. When Pip discovers Houdini escaped just after we left – and that he's still missing – she goes into meltdown. Dad is grovellingly apologetic.

'I locked his cage door like you showed me, Pip,' he sighs, running his fingers through his hair, which I'm sure has got tons more grey in it all of a sudden. 'I don't know how he did it, but next time I went to feed him the door was wide open and he was gone.'

'We've looked everywhere,' Digby, Dad's assistant backs him up. 'And we've left little dishes of food out so he won't go hungry. But we've just not managed to catch him.'

'We do know that he's fine, though,' Dad insists. 'The food has been disappearing.'

Pip is inconsolable. 'We've only been away for two days,' she wails. 'How could you have lost him?'

'Calm down, Pip,' I say, suddenly inspired. 'I know who can find him!'

Five minutes later Twig arrives at the door. 'Thank goodness you're here,' Pip says dramatically as she shows him in. 'Houdini's been missing FOR TWO WHOLE DAYS!'

'I'm sure he'll be fine,' Twig reassures her. 'Show me where his cage is, and we'll take it from there. OK?'

Pip leads Twig upstairs and shows him the empty cage. Then he goes into my room, and I'm thinking *oh no, here we go again* as he gets down on his hands and knees and looks under my bed.

Seconds later he sits up empty-handed.

Pip is rabbitting on about how Dad can't be trusted with anything when Twig clamps a hand over her mouth to shush her.

She stops mid-sentence. The room falls silent.

'Listen!' Twig urges.

And that's when I hear it. A tiny squeak. Followed by another, then several squeaks together.

'I don't understand,' I whisper. 'Is that Houdini?'

More squeaks come from under my bed. Pip gets down on her hands and knees and peeks under. Moments later she stands up, beaming.

'I'm a granny!' she squeals excitedly, just as Mum pokes her head round the door.

'A granny?' Mum asks, alarmed.

'Houdini's had babies!' Pip explains happily. 'Break open the champagne!'

'But Houdini's a BOY hamster,' Mum protests. 'We specifically asked the pet shop for a boy. BOYS can't have babies!'

'You'll need to call him Mrs Houdini now,' Twig laughs.

'She must have been pregnant when we got her,' Pip says. 'No wonder she was putting on weight!'

Mum shakes her head. 'I don't know, I leave your dad alone for two days . . . The hamster escapes, has a sex change, gets pregnant and gives birth. Thank goodness we took Brewster with us. Who knows what might have happened!'

At last Mum goes downstairs and Pip goes off to her room with Houdini and all his . . . er . . . *her* . . . babies. Twig flumps down on to my beanbag and looks at me in that quiet way that always makes me both thrilled and uncomfortable at once.

I pick up my guitar and strum it a few times, hoping he doesn't notice how nervous I feel.

'That song you sang at the festival,' Twig says slowly.

'Which song?' I ask, though I'm pretty sure I know which one he means.

'"Pinch Me, I Must Be Dreaming"?'

'Yeah?' I say, strumming the guitar gently.

'It's really good,' Twig says.

'Thanks,' I smile as I play the opening chords. 'I wrote it for someone pretty special. Would you like to hear it?'

Twig shakes his head and my hand stops mid-strum.

'Maybe later,' he smiles. 'But first I was wondering . . .'

My heart leaps into my throat. It seems so long since I made that wish on the first star.

'I was wondering . . .' Twig repeats. '. . . do you have a computer?'

I chuck Little Ted at him and he chucks a cushion at me, and then we're in a full-on pillow fight and Pip is shouting at us to keep quiet we're waking the babies and downstairs the phone is ringing and Twig's face is inches from mine, and then he kisses me and inside I'm singing, *Pinch me, I think I must be dreaming!*

LAST TRACK

You want to put barbed wire around my heart
You want to package me
To make me play a part
But I don't want to do those things for you.

So don't try to market me
Don't try to buy me out
Don't try to bribe me
With wealth and hollow dreams.

Cos I know what I will and will not do
I know what's right — I know what's true
I know that in this world
All's not always as it seems.

By Sassy Wilde

Get all the lowdown on

Maggi Gibson

Favourite book?

SCARLETT by Cathy Cassidy. It has everything I want in a book – great characters, funny bits, a terrific story – oh, and a dash of magic and romance.

Favourite song?

ONE LITTLE SONG by Gillian Welch. Not very well known, I know, but I love its simple lyrics and melody. Actually, I wish Sassy had written it.

Favourite film?

I love TEN THINGS I HATE ABOUT YOU. But I also adore LITTLE MISS SUNSHINE. It made me laugh so much I fell off the cinema seat and disgraced myself in front of my two daughters.

Favourite place in the world?

Balqhuidder (you say Bal-whid-der) in Scotland. I lived near there for a while. There are high mountains and two beautiful lochs. You have to go up a single track road to reach it and it all feels ancient and magical, like you might see fairies or ghosts at any minute. Cordelia would absolutely LOVE it!

Do you have a personal motto?

Only you can make your dreams come true!

Get all the latest news and gossip
from **Sassy** and her gang

at the megafab website:
seriouslysassy.co.uk

Sneaky peeks at **brand-new titles**

Details of fab **signings and events** near you

Write **your own song lyrics** and share them with friends

Post your **messages** to Maggi

Fun **competitions** and quizzes

Go on! Get sassy at
seriouslysassy.co.uk